The Enchanted Grandfather's Clock

by

Charlotte Jones

Illustrated by Parisa Jones

Share In the Magic of the Old Wooden Grandfather's Clock ~ I hope you enjoy the character's adventure your friend Charlotte Jones

Let the characters come to life & Enjoy this beautiful adventure created by my very own blessed mother, smile as you read this! X Parisa Jones!

Copyright

Butterfly Waterfall.

Land of Moon Dial.

Land of Cogs.

Land of Clock-face.

Land of Beveled Glass.

Cave of Bevel.

Key Lock

Land of Weights.

Mr & Mrs Pendulum.

Staircase of Memories.

The Time-Keepers Palace.

Dedication

For my daughter Parisa and for all children everywhere ...

... I am fearfully and wonderfully made: marvellous are thy works

Psalm 139 ~ verse 14

Find out more about Charlotte Jones by visiting her web sites at
http://charlottejonesauthor.co.uk and **www.facebook.com/charlottejonesauthor**

Contents

Chapter 1 - The Puzzling Problem

'Gem-Sun! Please, quickly get over here. Do look through my Telescope with urgency! One of the planets has disappeared. I am clearly not mistaken?' It was no ordinary day in this enchanted land. It was truly puzzling as one of the Gems who watched over distant lands through her golden telescope could not see the most important planet; she watched over them all every day. A whole planet missing!

Gem-Cloud was a beautiful creature I suppose I could describe her alike a pixie. She had the most delicate outfit that you have ever seen that was pleated down her body with folds of greyish blue and silver white chiffon. On her face she had a dainty cloud birth mark that added to her sweet heart shaped face. It glittered whenever she moved.

Gem-Cloud could see that the planets she looked onto through her golden telescope were not balanced in their usual place in the greater Universe. What was going on? She looked to the left and then she looked to the right. One planet was totally gone? Alarmed and perturbed Gem-Cloud called her sister with a sense of desperation. 'Gem-Sun, Do come quickly. It really is missing. A planet has gone!' She hoped she was wrong. Whenever Gem-Cloud got nervous she twiddled with her plaits that lay over her ears. Her hair was a masterpiece as it was short everywhere apart from where these two plaits flowed to her shoulders.

Gem-Sun quickly ran over to Gem-Cloud. She was in a beautiful orange gown that shone so brightly and with matching jewelled shining shoes. She also had a dazzling sun birth mark on her face that was just visible due to her excessively long blond hair that floated down. 'Are you certain about this Gem-Cloud? A planet is missing?'

As she stood tall before looking through the telescope she said, 'Gem-Cloud you clearly must be mistaken? That simply will not do. What nonsense in all the time we have governed the Land of Moon-Dial we have not had a planet go missing.' Gem-Sun didn't sound as though she was talking in an ordinary voice or tone. She 'sang' her words. That is correct. She completed her sentences in a musical tone and that is the way she always spoke and was loved for it.

Suddenly both Gem-Cloud and Gem-Sun were interrupted by their older sister.

'Missing? Hurry, let me look through your telescope so that I may see this puzzle for myself.'

Gem-Moon in her deeper blue chiffon outfit and short hair with ribbons in it was soon at Gem-Cloud's telescope looking outwards to the other planets. She looked through the golden telescope with huge magnification glass from the left to the right quickly. She moved it from the right to the left steadily. Yet again very slowly she moved the golden telescope from one side to the other.

'This is a very puzzling problem and we need to speak to Gem-Star with urgency.' She then started to count. 'One, two, three, four, five, six and eight.' She stood up with a jolt. 'Planet seven has disappeared, the planets shall soon be out of balance. This is treachery of some kind.'

Gem-Moon announced to her sisters in a worried voice, 'That Planet was home to a certain someone that was cast out of our time and home-lands for a very good reason. This must mean that he is preparing to return to our Land. We must act fast.' At that

Gem-Moon abandoned the telescope and went running off to speak to Gem-Star knowing that something miraculous was about to happen. Her younger sisters followed right behind her.

Chapter 2 - A Flamingo Pink Cottage

It was the boring, boring (I'll say it again just to make sure you got that point) totally boring summer holidays again. Six long wicked weeks without any of my friends to have fun times with and meanwhile my sister Emily who bores me and irritates me was at my Aunt Jane's cottage; the bright flamingo pink cottage. Aunt Jane by the way believes that her cottage it to be pale rose pink and that is because anything she believes to be true is true. Whilst waiting for my Mum downstairs I dazed into the huge mirror in the library. My brown hair was growing over my brown eyes and ears now and I liked it. Due to the sunshine my hair appeared to have streaks of redness through it and my freckles were on full show. Emily makes fun of my freckles when they come out with the sunshine but everyone knows they are a sign of real beauty. My Aunt Jane told me so and besides that Emily has more freckles than me!

Soon I would be joining my sister as Mum was packing her bags ready to visit our father who was working on important business overseas in America. Sunshine beamed in through the windows as I pondered over my last stay with Aunt Jane. Books, ginger biscuits, teapots and dandelions remind me of the last stay. Not forgetting the beautiful rivers and waterfalls in North Yorkshire and there were lots of those around to visit. I do think Aunt Jane tries her best to keep us busy at the cottage but I would like a few more friends to explore with you see. Plus a little bit of adventure. As a young Aunt she was rather unlike most of my friend's Aunties and she was quite different to her older sister (also known as my mother Julia). My mother always had such busy times in her life wishing and expressing that things would somehow always be better in the future. No more stress or rushing like crazy in the city would be in the future. Obviously this would be when my father no longer needed to work overseas and undoubtedly we would be grown up by then with our own families.

Aunt Jane is a little bit different to this or rather unusual compared to my mother. Mum likes to wear suits and smart outfits every day and her hair is dark, long, brown, straight and perfect with a very chic fringe. Blue, grey or black were her favourite colours to wear with bare look make-up. Aunt Jane on the other hand has crazy, long, curly light brown hair and has no fringe. She prefers dainty flowered printed dresses, boots, and zappy-tights, adores sunglasses most of the year and loves to wear lipstick.

'Make-up ensures that you feel better about yourself even on days when you don't feel at your best Jamie,' Aunt Jane often confirmed as she put on pink glossy lipstick.

In contrast to my home at Aunt Jane's cottage you get woke up at some ludicrous hour of the morning to ensure that each day was productive, fun and made the most of.

Often because, 'You never know what may happen tomorrow so enjoy joy and precious moments in the present today,' she would say to my sister and me. Such talk would take place whilst she baked ginger biscuits at six-thirty in the morning in her lavender painted kitchen.

Thank goodness we did not have to get dressed at that time. Most of my friends slept until ten-thirty in the holidays but with Aunt Jane chocolate-chip cookies or ginger biscuits would be served at that time after a full English breakfast at eight o'clock! Once when I was looking at stacks of teapots (Aunt Jane collects them you see) at the Teapot Shop in North Yorkshire I heard someone whispering to the cleaner that my Aunt Jane is eccentric. When I looked that word up in the dictionary eccentric I was rather surprised. Indeed I was and that is because the word 'eccentric' is defined as 'peculiar, odd, deviating from the normal and erratic. How amazed I was that this word truly describes my Aunt Jane perfectly. Here is a picture of my Aunt Jane with her collection of tea-pots!

My sister Emily who loves dolls and prams loves Aunt's kitchen and that's because it is so full of pretty things from bright coloured spotted cups on cute spotty trays, to delicate petals on wild white fresh flowers in a very elegant vase. Her vase is covered with butterflies and dragonflies flying upwards with coloured glass. Assembled over the fire place in the kitchen Aunt Jane has very cute photographs with her pet rabbits: Mischief Grey-Foot and Cinnamon-Nutmeg both who lived in the house and had their own private garden. Mischief was a lean black rabbit with very grey feet whilst Cinnamon-Nutmeg had the floppiest ears and often looked like a fluffy white ball in the garden. Believe it or not both of the rabbits had two houses in the gigantic garden. One home was a double bedroomed hutch (they love to sleep in this one) the second home was a fantastic children's playhouse fitted with carpets, curtains and food dishes inside. The neighbours think Aunt Jane is a bit 'different' and now you can understand why.

My quiet pondering thoughts were soon broken as my mother announced we were ready to leave,

'Jamie, do you have everything you need to take to Aunt Jane's cottage? We will be on our way now?'

I was all prepared and I just hoped nothing would be as boring as yesterday at home. I mean I do have good time reading my adventure comics in our home in the outskirts of London City. Yes, you are correct Reader. That is the place where we have Big Ben, Buckingham Palace, The Thames and The Underground. But with no friends in my neighbourhood to play with it is no fun at all. Believe me.

'I'm already set to go mother,' I replied.

I really wished my friends could have been with me for this trip. Emily so often would not get involved with the games I prefer you see and that meant we often would bicker and argue instead. What a waste of time. Apparently this bickering does happen between brothers and sisters (I'm sure you know what I am talking about) but not so often with two brothers. This was discussed in our last class before we broke up for the holiday season. My friends who are twin brothers are a fine example of this great friendship between brothers. Most of the time they read cartoon magazines or they spend their time tree climbing in the garden. They don't have time for bickering.

As we set off in my mother's gleaming white car she listened to the radio as she made her own humming tunes to the music. Meanwhile I day-dreamed about how when I was old enough with my own house I would like to have a swimming pool and lots of tree-houses. It would be a great place to hang-out and read comics. I certainly would not wear the boring clothes like the ones I wore at home; hideous shirts and trousers. No, no and no. T-shirts, trainers and jeans would be fine.

In my house I would have outstanding pets for good company. A few creatures like a tortoise I would name Mr Speedy, a spider I would name Charlotte (all children my age know the famous tale Charlotte's Web and if you don't I really do recommend it to you for reading) and my dogs: Toffee, Fudge and Caramel. These are the best sweets ever created!

Of course such a range of pets would mean they would have to live in different parts of my home. I would love my morning dog walks leaving Mr Speedy at home to munch on dandelions. Now that would be fantastic I would train the dogs in spectacular tricks and let them play up in my tree-house.

Obviously my tortoise would not ever be allowed to live in the tree-house as that would be far too unsafe for Mr Speedy, it would be a disaster if he fell from such a height! I would also not want my future pet Charlotte the huge spider to get eaten by my pet dogs or Mr Speedy the tortoise so I would keep my animals away from each other. Mr Speedy would not like to experience Charlotte the Super Spider climbing all over his shell.

My dream home would not be painted flamingo pink like Aunt Jane's cottage and it would be smaller and more fun than my own home. What is the point of a huge empty house? Mum and Dad bought us a house that now has six huge bedrooms. I love my home but so often my mother dedicated hours each day in cleaning it and then feeling very tired; she would never have a maid to do it instead. When I get older (currently I am ten years old) I do not want to spend all my time cleaning a huge house. Now that would be a waste of play and time that could be well spent. My house would be located next door to Thomas, who would live next to Aidan, who would live next to Josh. How ideal and that would be? So awesome! Fun times every day! There would be marble matches, card games and football. Most importantly we would get to play our favourite Marvel Comic characters and I would be Spiderman or Superman depending on what power was required for our hero to win against evil. In-between comics we would ensure a few climbs into the trees, do digs in the garden for treasure and camping out nights. My day dreams continued for most of the journey as my mother continued to sing quietly to herself as she drove. The time went quite quickly from parking up and eating our packed lunch on route up to North Yorkshire.

Soon my trail of thoughts was broken as I noticed that we were entering familiar roads into North Yorkshire and I recognised a huge mountain from a hill top our car was going to drive down. This was no ordinary huge mountain. Absolutely not! I just had to explain to my mother what I had found out on my last visit about this mountain.

'Mum, you see that huge mountain over there that drops off at one end? Do you see it Mum?'

'Yes I see it Jamie, but I can't stare at it and that is because I am driving down hill and ducks cross over the street lower down here.'

'Mum that is the place where the Great Giant was buried many hundreds of years ago because he had lived for such a long time. For thousands of years! The people of North Yorkshire wanted to keep his body and that is because he protected these lands from other Giant intruders.' My mother for the first time on the journey started to smile.

'Is that so Jamie? Could I just ask you where you heard that tale from?'

'Mum, it is not a tale and it is very true. If you don't believe me you just ask Aunt Jane and she will explain everything. He was the oldest Giant ever to exist. Apparently Mum he helped the villagers build houses, he went fishing in the sea for them at Whitby every week. Mum Whitby seaside is a few hours from here at least but according to Aunt Jane it was just a stroll out for the Great Giant.'

'Well he must have been quite gigantic to be buried underneath such a huge mountain,' my Mother pointed out.

Jamie explained, 'Well that is the thing you see, if you don't live here you would just think that it is just a massive mountain. Wouldn't you Mother? But Aunt Jane said everybody knows if they are a real villager (that means you live and were brought up in North Yorkshire) the true story. It is the Great Giant's grave. The villagers did not want to put a gravestone up for a good reason. It is because the Great Giant loves the land and he was happy for people to never know he was buried there and for them to climb up and picnic up there so he would always have friends around him.'

Before I could explain more about the Great Giant my mum had to stop the car. There was a picture sign to say that ducks crossing was to be expected. Two small rivers ran through the small village opposite sides of the main road with a few houses and only one pub. Ducks waddled across the road throughout the day whenever they decided they would like to swim on the other river for a change of scene. The mother duck of course kept the queue of ducklings in order turning to check each of them were following her instructions.

My Mother replied, 'Well I'm sure the Giant will be happy wherever he is Jamie; especially with all the sheep that climb over him every day!' I must ask Aunt Jane to tell me the exact dates of this tale happening.'

Then when the sweet ducklings passed we set off again intending to arrive at Aunt Jane's for mid-afternoon. I knew it wouldn't be long now until we reached Aunt Jane's house. We entered the village of Leyburn. Now this is quite a special place and that is because when my Aunt Jane was little she watched a programme called 'All Creatures Great and Small.' This programme had lots and lots of animals in it and Vets who looked after them all. I would love to watch this programme but it is not on television now. Aunt Jane on my first trip when I must have been very little told me how this programme was filmed in this local area. Local people allowed the camera crews and stars of the show to use their land or homes to make such a great show. Aunt Jane said that most of the pubs like The Golden Lion were the places the film crew would hang out with friends. They would get together on an evening for local Yorkshire puddings or Wensleydale cheese with crackers.

I love Yorkshire puddings and think it is very strange how in many places in the world today people do not eat Yorkshire Puddings on a Sunday. I think it should be made into a law. I cannot understand why anyone would not want to not eat Yorkshire Puddings on a Sunday?

My mum was giggling to herself in the car and I asked,

'Mum why are you giggling? What is funny?'

She replied,' Well, I'll tell you something about Aunt Jane. When she was studying at College about human biology and how we grow, her teacher once told her that in her experience of being a Nurse, she had cared for a Giant. Aunt Jane of course was the first one to find this very hilarious and amusing, thinking it was not at all possible. To nurse a Giant was ridiculous. She came home and shared with our family the teacher's talk and found it most interesting indeed. Anyhow, when Aunt Jane studied at St. Bartholomew's Nursing School in London she eventually learned that in fact the teacher was telling the truth.'

'Is that really true Mum? I could not believe what I was hearing!'

'Yes, Jamie it is true. She rang her teacher and apologised and that is because Aunt Jane's first patient was very special to her and in fact he was a Giant.'

'Mum, how do Giants become Giants? I enquired'

'Well Jamie,' she explained 'sometimes it can be most unfortunate as there is a part of the brain that encourages the person to keep growing and sometimes it is due to what we call a growth.'

I was amazed by this and was just so thankful that in the world today we have doctors and nurses who work their very best to make people get better. Perhaps I would read more about Giants at Aunt Jane's house during the holidays.

'Wow! I exclaimed. That is really amazing. I think I would be scared of a Giant even if he was a kind one!'

Lots of sheep were scattered on the fields and they looked like small cotton wool balls on the green grass. We continued onto the flamingo pink cottage. I would really like a pet lamb. Before I could think any more about where that pet would live I could see pink behind lots of green trees. We had arrived at Aunt Jane's home. As we climbed out of the car I ran over to the little stoned wall and bridge that you can look down over. There was the water rippling over the stones and greasy green weeds again. It looked no different from my last visit. No frogs were out today. I love frogs so I decided that if it rained I would revisit this spot to catch one. They would definitely be out and about in the rain.

Chapter 3 - One Extraordinary Clock

'Welcome, welcome once again my sweetie pie,' Aunt Jane delighted as she squeezed me to pieces.

I was finding it difficult to speak as I couldn't breathe as she squeezed me so tightly. My mother walked into the kitchen and dropped my bags through into the hall at the bottom of the staircase. Aunt Jane had paint on her forehead and as my mother flicked on the kettle switch for tea she laughed and asked her,

'What on earth have you being doing Jane to have silver paint on your head?'

Aunt Jane called for my sister to join us,

'Emily come down and carry that stencil with you my little munchkin your mother is here and we are having some tea!'

Emily came into the kitchen and had an apron on with silver paint all over her hands,

'Hi Mummy, I'm decorating Aunt Jane's room and that is because she could not do this without me and needed my help.' Emily smiled full of joy and pride.

'We are using an alphabetical stencil Mummy,' Emily beamed.

Aunt Jane replied, 'We are taking parts of my favourite poem and stencilling it around the walls in my bedroom for daily inspiration.'

Now this to me sounded very interesting indeed and I was just about to offer my help when Aunt Jane got out some of my favourite cheese scones from her floral baking tin. Aunt Jane served afternoon tea. Over the next hour my Mother and Aunt Jane discussed how she was flying overseas late at night and then shared our clothing items she had packed knowing we would be fine at the cottage over the rest of the summer holidays.

In exchange, Aunt Jane shared all the different fun things we would be doing in North Yorkshire. She was excited about us going strawberry picking as the local farms had beautiful crops. She was also taking us to a place called the 'Forbidden Corner.'

'It must be booked in advance as it is so popular children. It used to be a privately owned garden. Now it is an adventure ground to explore,' explained Aunt Jane.

'Wow, I said. I can't wait I love exploring Aunt Jane!'

Then Aunt Jane shared the North Yorkshire teapot trail. This would include her favourite carrot cake at Durant's team room for us to visit. Emily got really excited about our planned waterfall walks at Aysgarth Fall's and Hawes waterfall in North Yorkshire.

The most exciting thing that Aunt Jane mentioned was how she had found out about a cute little railway museum not too far from North Yorkshire. It was in a town called Darlington. According to Aunt Jane this is where the first railway was built from Darlington to Stockton.

'The train was called The Rocket,' she smiled.

Well you can imagine just how excited I was about this piece of news. I could not contain myself!

'Wow that will be amazing and great to see, I love trains Aunt Jane!' I approved.'

I was so glad to be at the cottage now and I could not wait for our trips out! Aunt Jane then added to this exciting piece of news,

'Recently this local town of Darlington have celebrated their success even more Jamie,' she explained. If you look on the back of a twenty-pound note, George Stevenson who created the first train 'Rocket' has his portrait printed on the back of the twenty-pound note. Not only that in the out-skirts of the town a red brick train model comes out of a real hillside.'

I was beaming now as at this point Aunt Jane took a pencil and doodled. She passed me a picture of what it looked like. Meanwhile my mother pulled her purse out of her handbag. She found a twenty pound note and sure enough, there on the back of it was George Stevenson with wavy hair and his achievement recognised. It was a purple bank note so of course in the diagram he was purple! He was on the other side to the queen's head on the paper note.

That one hour passed quickly with Aunt Jane and my Mother. Soon we were brought back to my mother needing to leave as Aunt Jane's Grandfather Clock chimed that it was five-o'clock. I forgot about that old clock of Aunt Jane's that she loved so dearly. When the clock sounded Aunt Jane touched her necklace chain and for the first time I noticed that her necklace had a tiny little bottle pendant on it. It was a glass bottle with something inside. Before I could ask her about it my mother jumped to her feet,

'Children it is time for me to go now. I'm going to miss you both so very much!' Emily ran around the wooden table to hug my mother and I stood up waiting for my turn.

Aunt Jane reassured my mother,

'Julia, you know they are both in very safe hands and how they will be well looked after. It's best that you set off now to ensure you are at the airport early for the check-in. It would be a disappointment if you were to miss your flight.'

Aunt Jane whispered to us both as we waved goodbye to the white gleaming car with my mum in it,

'We are going to have so much fun together and I've missed you both so much,' she kissed us both Emily and I on our heads.

Believe it or not it did take too long for Emily and I to forget Mum had gone for six weeks. In fact, I soon had silver paint on my hands and face too. We worked on the stencilling for another hour in Aunt Jane's room and we had a whale of a time mixing in the colours and helping stencil her inspiring words across the bedroom.

As Emily got bathed and ready for bed I went down to the kitchen for another cheese scone. The Grandfather's clock melody chimes started to ring as again as it was on the hour. As I munched the fluffy buttery scone I decided I wanted to take a look at it so I shuffled out of the kitchen with two cheese scones in hand and into the hall beneath the stairs. This Grandfather's clock fascinated me. It was so old looking, chipped and out of place in Aunt Jane's pretty cottage. Nothing matched it. It was so rickety and truly it did not match Aunt Jane's style. I am sure that one day many years ago this clock must have been a grand fixture of someone's home. The Grandfather's clock was at the bottom of the stairs, set back near the pine book case. It was not in Aunt Jane's comfortable lounge and I can imagine that is because of the noise it makes each hour. How on earth could you read or watch television?

A colourful, floral Persian carpet lay in front of the old clock and I decided to sit on it munching my cheese scones. I was waiting to watch the clock chime.

At the top of the Grandfather's clock it had two horn-type features with a centre piece that appeared like a miniature trophy. Now beneath this there were engraved wooden loops. Beneath these loops and in the depth of the clock; I could see something very bright. It was sparkling so much that it got me to stand up and walk towards the clock. I got closer and closer to peek at the clock to see where the light was coming from and I realised there were two objects that dazzled. Looking closer it was a sun and moon dial. The moon appeared to be moving in a clockwise direction whilst the sun moved around it in an anti-clockwise direction. They both sparkled. Suddenly my eyes dropped for a moment. That is when I noticed some letters engraved into the wood that went into a twirling pattern.

The words read, 'Gnoble,' Of course, I knew straight away that this 'Gnoble' must be the person who made the Grandfather's clock. As I touched the wooden panels of the clock I started to think of quite amazing things, like when I won the science invention competition at school and when I came second in the treasure hunt at scouts. I also remembered how I won the Marvel cartoon comic competition for my fantastic comic strip I entered. My hand kept against the wooden panel as I continued to look down into the clock. I looked at the middle of the clock and the empty lock that was in twirls of beautifully engraved wood. I watched the hanging golden pendulums swing overlapping each other inside the glass panel in the lower part of the clock. Music was playing and it had no words to it? I listened carefully as I was uncertain where it was coming from. The music was so beautiful and I could hear the rhythm of the clock in time with the music.

'Tick-Tock, Tick-Tock, Tick-Tock, Tick-Tock.'

'Jamie, are you enjoying my most precious Grandfather's clock and admiring it?' Aunt Jane enquired. 'It is rather beautiful isn't it?' Aunt Jane was stood right behind me and I jumped out of skin as I had no idea that she had been watching me. Or that she had come downstairs to find me. I must say that I did feel a little bit odd in that moment. I took my hand off the Grandfather's Clock wooden panelling.

'Aunt Jane, are you playing music somewhere upstairs,' I asked. At this point Aunt Jane gradually got close and started to kneel as she touched the panel of the wood on the clock.

'Do you hear music Jamie?' she questioned me quietly.

'I do Aunt Jane and it is lovely music too, I just have no idea as to how it started to play?'

Aunt Jane started to smile as her hand touched her necklace again, it was a slow unfolding smile and she then declared,

'It's not my music you can hear playing Jamie but if you hear music at any time then it must be from somewhere. Music is music and it is played to an audience to captivate their interest,' she explained.

Aunt Jane had the most twinkling eyes that you have ever seen before. Big, brown, almond shaped eyes that twinkled like sequins.

Then I remembered that this is usual for my Aunt Jane. She could be vague and quite bizarre at times.

I asked her, 'Aunt Jane, who is Gnoble?'

Aunt Jane at that point took a deep breath in almost like a gasp of surprise,

'Oh, my goodness sweetie, *Gnoble* is not a person. No absolutely not a person. My darling *Gnoble* is a place; a magnificent place.'

Now it was her turn to look as though she had drifted off somewhere in a trance.

'I've never heard of that place before Aunt Jane. Is it in England?'

Aunt Jane now was beaming with her chocolate brown eyes staring deeply into mine.

'No, no, no! It's not in England Jamie and I'm sure at some point you will learn more about this magnificent place but as for now it is time for bed,' Aunt Jane yawned.

Aunt Jane followed me upstairs and as I went into the spare bedroom and there was Emily snuggled with her Rupert bear asleep in her bed. Aunt Jane loved patchworks and the beds were covered with handmade patchwork quilts that she had stitched herself in pastel colours of blue, pink and purple. It was so cosy in this bedroom. After brushing my teeth and after a few splashes of water over my face I climbed into bed yawning, wearing my favourite Spiderman pyjamas. It had been an extremely long day.

Aunt Jane kissed me on the head as she tucked me in and said, 'I have a surprise for you when the lights are turned out.'

I was so dozy now that I couldn't imagine what would surprise me so late at night as I lay tucked up in bed. I wriggled around into a comfortable position and as I turned over I looked at the ceiling. There was the huge surprise in front of me. Illuminated night stars that came to life in the darkness were all over the ceiling. Aunt Jane had covered the ceiling in the spare bedroom with these magic stars. They were not visible during the day time.

'Wow,' I admitted closing my eyes. My Aunt Jane was a star.

Chapter 4 - With the Twist of a Key

The next morning I woke up to the smell of sweetness. The aroma drifted up the stairs and into our double bedroom. Emily and I shared the bedroom and I could see that she was waking up to the smell of delicious too.

'What a yummy smell,' I yawned throwing off the duvet quilt cover.

It was time to see what was going on in the kitchen. The slippers went on and I drifted in a hazy state downstairs. Just before I went into the kitchen at the bottom of the stairs I peeked at the old clock to find out the time and the two black dials indicated it was a quarter-past seven. The numbers on the clock were black and encased in golden circles. The full clock face was on a glitzed golden background in one larger circle containing all the numbers. I was just walking up to the clock again to look at the centre of the clock face as behind it appeared to have different colours and patterns when Aunt Jane popped around from the kitchen entrance.

'Good morning my dearest, are you fascinated by my old Grandfather Clock? Still find it interesting hey Jamie? Now then come inside the kitchen as you have overslept and it is time for some tea and breakfast.'

In the lavender painted kitchen Aunt Jane opened the dotty teapot lid and poured in teabags and hot water. She was the most interesting member of my family was Aunt Jane. Already she was up and dressed with a pretty top and skirt ready for the day ahead. As I sat she poured my tea into the dotty cup to match the teapot she smiled at me.

'Did you like my stars last night Mr Jamie or should I say my Jamester?'

She always called us cute names and that was usual for Aunt Jane. I'm sure she made the names up as she fancied.

'Aunt Jane, what is a Jamester? I asked.'

She smiled showing her lovely white pearly teeth, 'Easy answer to that question. A Jamester is a name for a nephew who I love dearly, who is lots of fun and cute that I only ever give this name, title and position to.'

Each time I saw Aunt Jane she always made me feel special, important and unlike any other person. Emily and I were her only niece and nephew as Aunt Jane had no children of her own. She lived alone. She once explained that she had so many hobbies, interests and work to keep her happy that she really did not mind. She was never lonely she said. Aunt Jane after making my cup of tea opened the oven door with her oven mitts on. It was time to take the ginger bread out of the oven.

'That smells really good Aunt Jane!' I announced.

She then decided it was time to wake up Emily. 'My little one has slept for longer than you Jamie so I'm sure she won't mind me waking her up now for breakfast.'

As Aunt Jane climbed upstairs to wake Emily, deep down inside I was sad as I enjoyed having time with Aunt Jane on my own. I know Emily is younger than me but she really got on my nerves sometimes and when I was doing special things at home she would interrupt me and spoil my fun. I would never ever tell anyone else how I felt as it is important to keep upset feelings to oneself as a brave lad. I certainly did not want to get into trouble with my parents for sharing how irritating my sister can be. Besides, whenever Emily and I had our battles she would always get away with or excused from her behaviour as she was the youngest. Often I got told I should know better. Emily at times could be a nightmare and I also asked my mum if at my birthday parties she didn't have to be there. She caused problems and made me look silly in front of my friends. At birthday events I only wanted my boy mates to be there from scouts and football. Emily always caused so much havoc.

One year Emily opened my gifts thinking they were for her and I'm sure she had done that on purpose. Lots of my friends said they have the same problem if they have a younger brother or sister. My friends who did not have a younger sibling said they never had a problem and I do wish sometimes I was the only child. You see, I was on my own for a few years before Emily arrived. She was a surprise for me to keep me company my parents said. One day after school I found that Emily had broken my favourite lollypop stick model that I had made into a gigantic jet plane. It was kept in my bedroom. My parents of course said that none of this was done on purpose. To me that was not the point as my model of the jet plane was very special to me and had taken lots of time and care to make. It was not fair that Emily had gone into my bedroom in the first place.

It was great news for me when our family friend had decided to drop Emily off the week before I arrived at Aunt Jane's cottage. This was so that Emily would settle in and give mum time to sort things out to go overseas. I know I was bored at home but I really truly liked not having Emily around. It was incredibly peaceful.

I poured myself another cup of tea into my dotty cup and was glad that no one knew how I felt about my little sister. I looked at the photographs that Aunt Jane had on her kitchen window sill. There was Aunt Jane smiling beaming teeth at one of her famous 'Pudding Parties' that she hosted every year without fail. The picture had Aunt Jane with rather spectacular puddings that she had created for her 'Pudding Party' guests. I smiled remembering how Aunt Jane loved her word searches and quizzes all to do with puddings. There would be pudding poetry and games all played at her pudding parties. It was Aunt Jane's traditional event.

'Aunt Jane,' I asked. 'What do you make for your pudding parties?' I yelled out knowing she would hear me.

She called down the stairs, 'Something baked, something iced, something different, something traditional, something fruitful, something with zest and something with chocolate.'

As I told you my Aunt Jane was a very interesting character.

Soon Aunt Jane and Emily came downstairs and joined me at breakfast. After cereal, soft-boiled eggs and soldiers we got some fruit, salad sandwiches and gingerbread into a hamper basket ready to start our outings in North Yorkshire. After a quick change of clothing we closed the cottage door and ran down the pathway. The sun rays beamed down onto Aunt Jane's cream convertible beetle car and not long after the hamper went into the tiny boot Aunt Jane opened up the car and we climbed into the passenger seats. The car roof was taken down.

'It's time for us to go and see the waterfalls at Aysgarth Falls. This is the location where one of the movies called Robin Hood was filmed recently. After the waterfalls we'll go up to the castle that Richard III used to live that is quite old and ruined at Middleham.'

I was so excited to be visiting all these fun places. As I sat in the car I started to hum a tune. I have no idea where it came from. It was the musical tune from the night before at the Old Grandfather's Clock.

Aunt Jane fastened her floral scarf around her neck, popped on her sunglasses and then zoom off we went. As young as Aunt Jane may be she really does like some older music. My tune went out of my mind as Aunt Jane put on some jazz music. She played an orchestral band and we listened to the band as we whirled through the roads in the countryside from Leyburn to Aysgarth in the V.W.Beetle.

'I love this band Glen Miller,' she shouted so we could hear her in the back of the car.

The wind was an amazing feeling as it blew your hair everywhere and in between we would have the sunshine and shadows of the trees. Along with the loud jazz music it was a really fun experience. I loved looking out at all of the greenery and sheep scattered all over the fields. Some sheep had a black dot on them and then some of them didn't have a black dot. The cows and horses looked happy as they grazed on the grass whichever field they were in.

Aunt Jane started to shout out loud so we could hear her over the loud music,

'You see the thing I really loved about the cows in North Yorkshire is that they have the most beautiful eye-lashes. I am pretty certain that all of those Moos in North Yorkshire wake up first thing on a morning and put on lots of eye mascara. Just so it makes their eyes look so beautiful and big.'

Emily and I laughed as we knew how our mother loved to wear eye mascara but the thought of cows putting it on like Aunt Jane suggested was just such nonsense and fun.

After going through a tiny little village at slow speed Aunt Jane turned the beetle around the corner and half way down the hill she pulled the car around into a car park.

'Here we are munchkins. Now then, they have a cute little shop we can call in at but that will be after we have visited the waterfalls. I would like to walk around the falls and show you where the film was made.'

She put the roof back up over the car and pulled out the hamper basket. Emily was jumping around in her bright pink outfit whilst I was put in charge of carrying the hamper basket. It was a beautiful place at Aysgarth Falls. The water rippled over the stones in the river whilst the trees dipped over and into the water. The trees reached out over all the riverside. The water was not too high and many children and parents had their feet in the river if not their full bodies! We agreed to dangle our feet into the water as we looked out for fish. Aunt Jane explained precisely where at the upper falls the film Robin Hood and the Prince of Thieves was filmed. We pretended to be the merry men hiding behind the trees like bushes like they did in the movie. I loved every minute of this.

The facts of these triple-waterfalls were so interesting, 'Aunt Jane, I would love to have my own tree-house and home in these grounds. Do you think that would be possible?'

'No Jamie dearest it would not be. These areas are protected and a part of a National Trust,' she explained.

'Wow, gallons of water ripple over these rock ledges Aunt Jane,' I pointed out.

'You are quite right Jamie and I hope people will continue to protect these places in England,' she exclaimed.

Soon enough it was lunch time and the patterned blanket was put under the tree by the falls whilst we enjoyed our light lunch followed by home baked gingerbread. Cartons of juice were soon polished off and we packed up the rubbish ready to go for another walk. We went to another waterfall. In my mind as I walked I could hear the music again from the Grandfather's Clock.

'Tick-Tock, Tick-Tock'

I started to hum the tune. Aunt Jane chatted about how she loved the wildlife here and that walking by the falls was really good fun. Then she stopped as she noticed I was humming my tune from the Grandfather's Clock.

'That is a very lovely tune you are singing Jamie,' she told me.

'I think I may have heard that tune somewhere before?' Aunt Jane puzzled.

Then I saw how Aunt Jane was fiddling with the little bottle on her necklace so I decided to ask her about it.

'Aunt Jane, does that bottle have something inside of it? You know the bottle I mean. That bottle on your necklace?'

She smiled at me. 'It does indeed Jamester; it has a little note inside of it from a special friend.'

At this point Emily started to giggle and I joined her. 'Aunt Jane, that bottle is so small with a message inside of it? Well that message must be on the tiniest piece of paper ever! Aunt Jane, How on earth could any friend write a message and put it into such a small bottle like that? How do you read the message?'

I wailed whilst trying to hold my laughter in. Aunt Jane stood up. She was still smiling as she picked up the hamper basket ready for us to leave.

'Well my little nephew, you asked me about my necklace and I have told you the truth. If you want to make my answer totally ridiculous then that is up to you. All I will say is that it is a very special message and it is not for anyone to know or read about. The fact is it is my favourite possession and yes it seems quite odd but the fact is it suits me perfectly well.'

Emily and I giggled as we enjoyed the scenery as we marched down the hills to go to the trinket shop. We both browsed and got some pencils for school friends before we set off in the V.W. Beetle again to Middleham, North Yorkshire.

The weather remained beautiful all day and after travelling over the windy roads in a new direction, over a one way road we soon arrived at Middleham. It was a very small little village with a cobbled square that was right in the centre besides a monument. Aunt Jane pointed out to us her favourite tearoom that sold amazing jams called Durant's tea room where we would be going later. Then she walked us up to the old ruins where Richard III had history to this ruined castle. Aunt Jane opened her English Heritage map up and started to explain to us how at one stage King Edward was held as a prisoner at Middleham Castle. It was such good fun running around the ruins and pretending that it was my own castle.

The cows in the fields kept looking over with their long eye-lashes until they got taken away by the farmhand. It was possibly time for them to produce some more delicious Wensleydale milk for cheese. Now something quite odd happened when I was hiding in the castle. I was hidden behind a stone ruin and I heard a female voice speak out.

'The victory will be yours Jamie!'

I turned to see where this voice was coming from and I could not see anyone around me that could have said this to me. I thought about it. Perhaps someone else was called Jamie? It may not have been me that the female was speaking to? How odd? Nobody was in sight.

Believe it or not all of the fun at the castle did make Emily and I very thirsty. What was great about being thirsty from running around the castle pretending we were at battle with each other is that Aunt Jane took us into Durant's tea room for drinks. Inside the tea room the three of us climbed the little stairs and sat in the little room where they served us tea. The place was filled with beautiful pictures and lots of North Yorkshire made goodies. These included: caramel apple pie, carrot cake, chocolate cake and coffee with walnut slices. It was fantastic at Durrants!

'Aunt Jane, you simply must take us on more Teapot Trails in North Yorkshire!' I said munching through my carrot cake.

'Of course I will Jamie,' Aunt Jane agreed.

I then explained to Aunt Jane as she munched her chocolate cake how in the castle I thought I heard a lady speaking to me. Aunt Jane stopped eating her chocolate cake.

'What did she say to you Jamie?'

I told Aunt Jane, 'the voice said the victory will be yours Jamie.'

Aunt Jane nodded and left the rest of her chocolate cake. She said we needed to get back to the cottage as soon as possible without giving any reason.

After such an active day and lots of running around it was time to say farewell to Middleham and the delicious tea-room. After climbing into the V.W.Beetle we zoomed off back to the flamingo pink cottage. When Aunt Jane turned around the corners on the roads Emily and I flew from one side of the car (yes even with our seat belts on) to the other and that is because the roads were just so windy and Aunt Jane was driving like crazy!

Soon we were back at the cottage and I was getting ready for a hot drink before bed. Upstairs Aunt Jane read to Emily in the bedroom (I was allowed to stay up for one hour extra past her bedtime you see) as I scooped out the chocolate from the bottom of my mug.

Yet again I found myself sitting in front of the old Grandfather's clock. I love drawing and I decided to draw the clock and to practise my pencil drawings. Now what was really unusual is as I started to draw this Grandfather's clock I noticed that something had changed. I wasn't quite sure of what had changed; it was only yesterday that I was stood right before it. I suppose it is a similar situation to when you are looking at a friend who looks different, a friend that you know. Suddenly you realise that they have had a different hair cut or even had their ears pierced but it takes a while for you to notice. Well, that is the situation I found myself in right now.

I carried on drawing trying to figure things out as I doodled away on my art pad. Then I got it. My eyes dropped to the middle of the Grandfather's clock. A key stuck out of the Grandfather clock's door. It was so obvious in front of me now. I know I was not imagining things and that is because that same key was for sure not there last night. I jumped to my feet and took a closer look at it in the middle part of the clock.

Now this was strange and that is because the key was in the door of the clock and locked tight when I tried to use it to pull the Grandfather's clock door open. Although it was old the key had the most glorious patterned loops on it that looked a bit out of place because it was really quite big sticking out of the door. It almost looked like it belonged to a much bigger door because it had such big thickened loops quite huge in comparison to the size of the lock.

I must add how I was a bit disappointed that the door wouldn't open. I just so wanted to see the insides of the clock and had no doubts that it would be splendid inside. Lots and lots of different parts. My inquisitiveness was put to a stop when the telephone started to ring in the hall.

'Jamie. Darling! Would you pick that telephone up for me as Emily is sleeping? Ever so quickly pick it up for me,' Aunt Jane requested.

As I did, Aunt Jane came sweeping down the stairs and then she quickly took the phone from me with a big smile before I could even say Hello. By Aunt Jane's face I knew there was something not right. She never frowned intensely and her smile disappeared. She put her hand over her mouth looking stunned and upset. She just listened to the person who was speaking to her.

Little words, 'Hmm and I see or I understand,' Aunt Jane mumbled.

I just sat on the Persian carpet whilst Aunt Jane sat on the chair by the telephone. Eventually Aunt Jane said something important.

'Don't worry Ben, I'll watch the children and there are no issues at my end. You have nothing to worry about here. You just do whatever you need to do over there and keep me updated.'

I could see that Aunt Jane had tears in her eyes when she said, 'I love you both so much and tell Julia I love her very much and not to worry.'

Aunt Jane put the phone down and took me into the kitchen for a refill of my hot drink and I knew she was going to tell me something serious. During my hot chocolate Aunt Jane explained,

'Your mother has taken ill Jamie. Your Father has taken her to the doctors and due to her having a temperature, headaches and fainting so suddenly she had to be admitted into the hospital for investigations.'

Aunt Jane continued,

'The doctors are concerned because they did not think that the travel, flight or climate had anything to do with the condition she has presented with.' I could tell that my Aunt Jane did not want to worry me but at the same time knew she had to tell me something. She knew I heard Dad's speaking to her on the telephone.

Aunt Jane then started to talk to me in a vague way. She had not spoken to me like this before.

'Jamie, can you be brave for me? We must be very careful at this moment in time and not say too much to Emily to distress her. But can you be brave?'

I answered, 'Of course I can be brave and I wouldn't say anything to upset Emily.'

Aunt Jane explained, 'Jamie, sometimes in situations like this we have to become brave. We have to face things in ourselves that make us weak even things we don't think make us weak like selfish thoughts. We are more powerful in love or when we give to others.

She added, 'It limits you and holds you back. Keeps you stuck in time and we must overcome such thoughts.'

I was slightly confused but nodded my head in agreement. Aunt Jane's eyes were glazed over and fixated on her cup of hot chocolate. She then lifted her eyes to look at me.

'If there is any part of you like that I am sure you will overcome it. At this time, right now in the moment you must do your best. Don't save it for tomorrow or the week after. Precious values are like jewels to give, to love and to enjoy. Precious moments bring joy Jamie and the best kind comes from serving others first, I serve you children first because you need me. Right now we will enjoy each moment together.'

Aunt Jane then picked me up. Yes I am much taller than Emily but indeed she picked me up and hugged me so much that I thought I would stop breathing. Upstairs I shuffled around on my pillows as Aunt Jane tucked me into bed. She stayed and watched over me and then just before I drifted off to sleep I heard Aunt Jane whispering something into my ear.

'Our real task is to overcome our biggest fears. They hold us back in time; fear keeps us stuck. Always remember that you are wonderful and capable of great change Jamie. You have all the resources inside you my sweet child.'

I felt so cosy and warm that I was unsure if Aunt Jane mentioned anything else as I fell asleep under the ceiling of stars.

Still today I'm uncertain of the reasons of why I woke up at such a ridiculous hour in the night. Unsure of what time it was and knowing how restless and uncomfortable I was feeling I drifted down the stairs without waking Aunt Jane or Emily. Admittedly my thoughts were a mixture before going to sleep thinking about my mother in hospital. Then I drifted to the magical waterfalls we had visited. I dreamed a little about the stars on my bedroom ceiling.

Now I was awake. Perhaps counting sheep would have been a better idea. In my pyjama nightwear I decided to make myself a warm drink as I knew that would be kinder than waking everyone up. I was so surprised to see that I had only slept for two and a half hours. That was dreadful news to see the Grandfather's Clock face at eleven-forty five. It made me feel more tired. Even worse more unsettled.

After I started to slurp my delicious hot chocolate I sat in the comfortable chair by the bookshelf under the stair case. I watched the clock as it kept ticking away and felt very cosy sat in that chair with the sound of the clock keeping me company. It was soon to be midnight and obviously knowing Aunt Jane would have us awake early for another entertaining day I felt it would be wise to return to bed. It was during that thought when suddenly everything changed for me. The key looked different! As I was approaching the stair case just before midnight I could hear that beautiful music again.

'Tick-Tock, Tick-Tock. Tick-Tock, Tick-Tock.'

I could hear it that music playing and that key. Why was it not there when I first looked at the clock? The key appeared to be much brighter and sparkling in the door lock. I decided before creeping back to bed that I would stay to watch the clock strike midnight. I was incredibly keen to see inside that clock so I waited for the clock to strike midnight so that I could watch what happened inside the clock when it chimed. The music was softly playing as I listened to the melody. Then I held onto the Grandfather Clock key. Once again I tried the lock with the twist of the key to see if I could take a look inside it.

The Grandfather's clock struck midnight; the beautiful music was getting louder and all I could see was spirals and spirals of multi-coloured rainbows. They wrapped around the whole of my body. My whole body was feeling pressure all over (a bit like being hoovered up or blow-dried by a gigantic hair dryer). As the rainbows spiralled and the music got louder, I could feel the key twisting in the lock of the Grandfather's clock door.

'Whoosh. Whoop. Whoosh. Whoop. Whoosh. Whoop. Whoosh. Tick-Tock, Tick-Tock, Tick-Tock.'

'Whoosh. Whoop. Whoosh. Whoop. Whoosh. Whoop. Whoosh. Tick-Tock, Tick-Tock, Tick-Tock.'

At this moment I had to close my eyes. Everything was so bright I could not keep them open a moment longer. I could feel myself falling over backwards. Bump. I had fallen onto the floor. It felt safer now that I was on the floor not feeling like I was stuck in a hoover machine. I could no longer feel the key in my hand. On the ground it was much safer than standing up. I ever so slowly started to open my eyes again. The music was still playing loudly and the pressure against the whole of my body had now stopped. Opening my eyes incredibly slowly I soon realised there were no more rainbow spirals.

'My goodness!' I yelled.

You have no idea what happened. I got the biggest shock of my life. Never mind rainbows!

Chapter 5 - An Unusual Event

I was inside what I would describe as a gigantic gold and wooden palace?

'Gosh!' I whimpered.

I noticed I was still wearing my pyjamas from bedtime in a place like this it did not seem quite right! I say palace and that is because it was a magnificent place. There were beautiful patterned robes over huge glass windows, fine chandeliers that were extravagant and fancy. I walked to a table that was set out for dining. Golden goblets on the table were very flash. The goblets were made out of a spiral that opened up for you to drink from and they were so delicately made I was unsure of how you could drink from one? All of the knives and forks were made of gold and the plates were beautifully made to match the goblets out of golden spirals. I continued to look around this most lovely place. The palace was no comparison to places I had visited before. By the way that includes Buckingham Palace. Then I saw it. It was the most glorious beautiful golden chair with intricate twirls and numbers over it. I walked towards the chair knowing I just had to take a closer look at this fascinating masterpiece. It was so deep and fabulous I had to try sitting in it. Just to see what it would be like.

'This is what it must be like to be a Royal!' I declared like a true Prince.

Frilly steps made of jewels lead from the wooden ground up towards the chair on a multi-coloured jewelled platform.

'Wow,' I gasped looking at the gorgeous decorations on the walls and ceilings. I placed my hand on the wooden walls because they had prints of golden numbers almost like a wall-paper. As I did this, I started to remember when I learned to ride my bike. Touching the wooden walls made me feel incredibly warm inside. My thoughts pondered back to my bike and the special times I had with my family. One experience was not too long ago but I really truly had such a time riding that bike. I took my hand from the wooden wall with the printed numbers and turned my head to look out of the window besides me.

'Grass?' I wondered. 'Or is it a field?' I queried as I looked out of the window. Suddenly my thoughts were totally on the outside of the palace as I noticed there was some fresh long gliding grass.

'So there is more to this place that just this room then!'

I hoped someone would listen to me. I walked down the jewelled steps so I could see more out of the curtained windows. Plenty of grass and it was deep, fresh, green grass. Now this got my attention. I was certain that there were flowers?

'Gosh. This place is amazing!' I was so eager to explore. It was just too bizarre for words. As I walked I then came to a huge door with a huge golden door handle. Now you must understand I was just so curious. I really had to go outside to explore so I then opened the door. I was dumb-founded. There in the middle of this garden was a party of some kind? I could hear soft music and there was an enormous golden marquee with numbers all over it in. I could hear countless voices coming from the marquee just above the soft music playing. I found myself running towards the marquee tent covered with numbers. Now right outside the tent after taking a few breaths I could not resist anymore. I stuck my head in low down to peek inside the tent to see exactly what was going on. The soft music had stopped playing.

Inside there was the most beautiful pale skinned lady on the stage in the front of a rather huge audience. She caught my attention immediately. She had deep red lips, dark brown eyes and her wavy brown hair was falling down to right past her waist. She appeared to be wearing some type of crown on her head that was golden and twinkling. I was drawn to take a much closer look but before I could even think about it she started to speak to the guests inside the marquee. I kept low and hid behind the largest chair I could find. There were such a range of fancy chairs as much so as there were a range of different shaped guests. All sizes from short, medium to large. Looking around these guests appeared quite odd. Nobody could see me so I just kept myself low and listened.

'My dearest fellows and most deliberate followers of our Time-Keeper's way. I thank you graciously for taking the time to be in my presence so that I may share with you some most pleasing news; there is still hope for our Enchanted Land of Bong and its' followers.'

I gasped. Did she just say Enchanted? I peeked through the gaps between the large chairs to listen carefully to what was going on.

As she walked slowly over the stage, her long white gown that had a golden sash with a ruffled trail followed her.

'For many of you who remember and I am sure many of you will it has been some time ago since you have been summoned to visit me from afar. I thank you all again as I inform you today that our Enchanted 'Key' has been unlocked for our attention. We all understand and know what this means for us. Do we or do we not?'

I could see lots of peculiar guests nodding their heads in agreement as she continued to gracefully walk on the stage. It was astonishing how the audience were captivated by their speaker. They stayed silent until she repeated the same question,

'Do we or do we not?'

At this point a very short chap stood up and it was difficult to see clearly but he appeared to have an outfit made out of watches? He spoke in quite a slow steady tone and as he turned I could see he had goggles on top of his head.

'Our radiant and kindest Time-Keeper. Our way teaches us that in such circumstances that we must meet the requirements of the greatest challenge of all, 'The Challenge of Chime.'

He then sat down as the audience started whispering and making comments about it being that time or how each puzzle takes time? I had no idea about any of this business but I was intrigued by the lovely speaker.

At that time the radiant one (I think she is known as the Time-Keeper?) declared,

'Dearest Watcher, you are so fine, precise and correct. 'Indeed, 'The Challenge of Chime' is before us and for another to be called upon in order to complete this task. The 'Challenge of Chime' means only one thing. Our Land of Enchantment must be prepared for the times ahead. We know what the consequences are. Do we or do we not? If we are unprepared or if the Challenge of Chime is not our success or won by our opponent?'

A rather pretty, pixie lady with purple hair (it looked like she'd had a terrible shock as it stood on end upwards) dressed in an outfit created from sparkling jewels stood up.

'My Grace, the ways we follow teach us that the whole of time will stand still. Not just in our Land of Bong but in other universes that the eye may not see but only dream about. There would be nothingness and no hope for all.'

Now what was really quite amazing about this pixie creature is that as she talked to the Time-keeper, her hair changed to a different colour! It was now Emerald Green and then Sapphire Blue. It was such a thing to see. It was like she swapped into different coloured wigs every few minutes.

The Time-Keeper nodded and agreed, 'You are only too right my beloved Gem-Star. I know you have always cared for our external universes as much as our own. You see all of us as one and bring such harmony to all lands.'

After watching Gem-Star's hair colour change from Ruby Red to White Sparkling Diamond, I suddenly started to digest the response she gave to the Time-Keeper. This information sounded pretty worrying to me. All of time to stand still? For all worlds to be in a state of nothingness? Surely that would have nothing to do with my home in England? I continued to listen.

Another member of the audience stood up next and he had the most unfamiliar shape. He had a huge chest and a huge behind. His nose was so long and curled. His shape reminded me of a teapot; especially when he put his hands on his huge waist.

'My most noble Time-Keeper,' he said in a squeaky voice. Now I was stunned. What an unbelievable surprise. The gowned Time-Keeper was noble? Was the Time-Keeper was a Royal Queen? I listened to him.

'It is known that when the Key is unlocked it can only occur if there needs to be learning in another. A life that learns lessons through the challenges faced. This learning can only be faced through the Challenge of Chime and must happen to enable them to return to their home.'

The Time-Keeper touched her crown and thanked him,

'Snuggle-Button, you are remarkably aware of our ways and it gives me pleasure to see you here today once more.'

The Time-Keeper engaged the audience and hooked them in her presence. As she thanked the Snuggle-Button his nose was wriggling all over the place in delight. I saw a few more creatures that looked the same as the Snuggle-Button with long pink noses. Each nose was wriggling around and there were quite a lot of high pitched squeals from that table compared to the other tables.

'It is now that I call upon the one who has been brought here today and must face the Challenge of Chime according to the ancient ways as recorded historically for our Enchanted Land of Bong. I would like you to greet our Guest and Chosen One who comes from outside our Enchanted Land of Bong. He has just arrived in our time to join us for great challenges ahead,' announced the Time-keeper.

I was interested to see who this guest was as I looked around the room to see who was going to stand up.

'Welcome Jamie, please would you join me?' she asked.

SHOCK! Me? Did she just mention my name? I was speechless now and started to quiver. Did the adorable fairy-like queen mean me?

Of course she did as everyone in the room started to look in my direction as though they knew I was there all along. That is when I really got the shakes and I don't know how I managed to put one foot in front of the other.

'Come up here Jamie! Our Guest! We are pleased to welcome you,' she declared.

Was she was calling me to the stage in front of this audience? How on earth did she know I was even in that Marquee Tent? I was behind the largest chair and nobody could have seen me. My tummy had butterflies. Not just fluttering butterflies but high-speed flying butterflies.

As I walked down the centre of the Marquee in-between hundreds of chairs these different characters applauded me and I was becoming even more nervous. My whole self was unsteady. As I approached the stage I noticed that the Time-Keeper's brown eyes never left me throughout this time. I didn't want to stare back at the Time-Keeper but she was so elegant and bewitching. Her golden headband was sculpted into the most unusual shapes of circles almost like wheels. I couldn't help but ask immediately,

'Miss Time-Keeper. Are those wheels on your crown?' She beamed the most beautiful smile.

'Welcome Jamie and thank you for your journey. Indeed my crown has circles but they are not exactly that. Do you see that they have little parts missing around them?'

I nodded still feeling overwhelmed by everything.

'My crown is the Crown of Cogs. It is a dedicated Crown that has been passed down to me as the dedicated Time-Keeper.'

I could not help but notice how lovely the Time-Keeper smelled. Freshness and sweetness is all I could smell. The scent was how I smell after a bath full of lovely perfumed bubbles. It was then when she turned to stand back the audience that I caught sight of the numbers in glittering black all over her golden sash. As she moved I could see the number three or the number four become more obvious on her gown. She waved her arms in the arm and the audience settled down once again. They sat down in their chairs.

How unusual are these people in this audience? I thought.

From the stage I could now see that each and every character was grouped across the room. The man with the extra-long nose was sitting with a lady who had an even longer nose. They were sitting with children who all had truly long noses. They were the ones making the squeaky noises.

In the corner I could see that there were a group of guests who looked like they were made of glass? They shined in the light of the marquee and looked like an empty glass bottle? They had very sharp peaks, like triangles on their heads. I imagined it would be rather uncomfortable in those outfits to move around or to sit down on this occasion.

The Time-Keeper now addressed this group of guests and asked them,

'Dearest sparkling Smithereens! Welcome again! Please share with our audience another matter of importance that has not yet been discussed. What do we know for certain is expected when our Key is unlocked?'

A most dainty twinkling child stood up. She had a frock that was made of glass droplets and in her ears she had matching pretty glass droplets as earrings.

'Our Grace, we all know that when the Key is opened by another, in another Universe that this action also allows the known enemy to our Enchanted Land of Bong to return. He is amongst us in our home lands now. In our childhood tales we have been told of his wicked selfish deeds and how he has performed such evil on our families that we must all be alert. To be aware he is here and his lack of loyalty. He has power when he is inside our Land to steal time, distract us and to cause chaos. He is miserable from his own deeds. He is motivated by greed and power!'

The sweet child was applauded and then she somehow managed to sit back down in the glass droplet dress.

Let me tell you this. I was feeling incredibly angst and nervous at this point as you can well imagine. Yes I was a guest and this party seemed really nice. Until right now I had no idea that a wicked, selfish evil enemy existed in such a lovely place!

The Time-Keeper sensing my anxious behaviour and thoughts stepped towards me and touched my shoulder. I really started to feel warm inside from down low in my tip toes right up to the top of my head. I experienced the feeling of peace and ease. She started to speak,

'We must be aware of his past evil so we have wisdom. Not for us to lose our focus especially for Jamie who must complete the Challenge of Chime.'

Now I really did feel awkward but the Time-Keeper continued on.

'We must be prepared now that our Key has been twisted allowing Jamie to join us. Preparation for you all is essential. When you return to your Lands you must be ready for the challenges. Preparation and determination is the key to mastery during the challenge. To be on our guard, you all know your homelands and your gifts. You know how they function and you know what is required. Together we can ensure that the Challenge of Chime is completed regardless of our enemy. We can and will have victory if we all follow our ancient way and are not tempted by any empty promises that the Time-Taker offers to us.

We all know too well the Time-Taker's schemes. How in the moment those promises appear great if not magnificent. Yet many here today from our Enchanted Land know how gratification or greed is tragic. We must not be selfish. We know how the immediate desires for fulfilment can be destructive.'

In the corner of the room I could see some huge brown furry ball like creatures; they appeared a bit bear-like. They had such short ears a bit like guinea-pigs but they were really round with a long tail. I say that because as they moved they didn't hop they appeared to roll? I noticed that one of them started to cry and that is because one of the other furry creatures passed a gigantic tissue to dry their tears. The Time-Keeper noticed this and spoke with softness.

'My dearest Fur-Fogs, you are now more prepared than all of us. If it were not for your honest discipline and effort in working so hard in the Land of Cogs, none of us would be here today. We know all your family has lost and your family's sacrifice. We value you and thank you for your bravery in the past. All of us know the lessons we must learn from our past experiences in our Enchanted Land.'

At this time I realised that one of the Fur-Fogs that had been crying started to smile through its tears at the Time-Keeper.

In the midst of this I had no idea whatsoever what all these stories and riddles were about. I did feel curious about the Challenge of Chime and all of these creatures. Then the Time-Keeper started to speak to me in front of the crowd.

'Jamie welcome to the Enchanted Land of Bong. We welcome you and honour you as our friend who according to our ways has been chosen with the Twist of a Key to enter our homelands.'

The audience cheered and clapped.

'We shall share with you as much knowledge as you need before you commence the Challenge of Chime but we must ensure that we do not waste time that is not ours to lose. You are here for a purpose and each moment is precious.'

More cheers and gladness was sounded by the audience.

'We shall eat together to celebrate Jamie's arrival and then as you friends are aware our Challenge must start as the Moon-Dial rises.'

The Time-Keeper took me to the banquet table inside the tent and kept me at her side as drinks and the most delicious foods were served by these feathered creatures. What was amazing about these creatures is that not one of them was the same colour. They had the most beautiful wings folded downwards so that they didn't knock anyone over. Pink, orange, blue, green, purple, red, black, brown, yellow and I could go on. They almost looked like birds but along with their wings they had feathery arms and legs. Six in total.

One of these feathery friends served me and introduced themselves in a very squawky voice,

'How do you do our Chosen Guest. My name is Orange (and yes indeed she was orange) and I am from the family of Plumage. Over there we have my parents Red and Yellow Plumage. They are with sat with my Aunts and Uncles, sisters, cousins and half-cousins.'

It only took a minute to realise that each bird was named after their colour.

'How rare are these birds?' I said delighted.

Before I could ponder any further Orange spoke to me.

'Sir Jamie, O Chosen One. I offer you my most precious tail feather. If you keep this with you in your pocket you can use it to call upon me if you need my help through the Challenge of Chime.'

'Thank you Orange,' I replied as I put the feather into my pyjama pocket.

Orange assured me that throughout the Challenge if I lifted the feather into the air, it would signal her to come to me. After talking to Orange I soon decided that my sister would love a Plumage instead of dolls. Orange served lots of food very fast indeed with those extra arms! All of the food was delicious and really quite tasty. Nothing looked like our food at home or like Aunt Jane's ginger pretty shaped biscuits but it tasted delicious.

When I was eating the Time-Keeper mentioned to me how I would throughout the Challenge of Chime meet her remarkable friends again as they came from the Lands where challenges were to be completed.

She explained how in each Land I faced a different challenge that I needed to accomplish. They would not be the same as the challenges completed before. Passing the challenge would then enable me to enter another Land.

To see all these friendly creatures again was a reassuring bit of information as you can imagine. I did not really want to do the challenges totally on my own. I tried to think how in some ways it would be a little bit like scouts.

All guests seemed incredibly nice and friendly. The Time-Keeper also said to me over dinner,

'The Challenge of Chime has been successfully in the past Jamie. I trust in you.' That little bit of information helped me to feel more positive about the Challenge of Chime.

Now this next part is really exciting. Honest. You won't believe what happened next. The Time-Keeper waved her fingers up in the air with her beautiful pale skin sparkling in the light of the Smithereens who were sitting next to use at the dinner table. She continued to wave her fingers up in the air and then a cloud bubble was created. It was floating in the air.

The Time-Keeper said, 'This is a map of the Land of Bong Jamie.'

The map identified many different Lands contained in Bong. Each part of the map was on its own inside the bubble. Then the Time-keeper repeated her fingers being circled around in the air. All of the Lands came together on the map in one piece.

I could not help but realise the shape of the Lands together on this map. The outline of the Land of Bong was sparkling in Golden light. It was the exact shape of the Grandfather's Clock! Yes. The words fell out of my mouth.

'Am I inside the Grandfather's Clock? Have I shrunk to get inside this clock? Do I look the same size?'

The Time-Keeper smiled. She glowed as her long brown wavy hair shaped her face. Her pale skin was so silky like one of Emily's dolls. She was like a real-life doll.

'Of course you are inside our Land of Bong. This is where you are right now Jamie.'

She pointed to the lower base of the clock, to the very bottom of the lower clock structure.

'The Challenge of Chime goes throughout the Land of Bong and she slowly pointed in a windy direction up to the very top part of the Grandfather's Clock. She pointed to the sparkling moon and sun dial of the clock. Her finger stopped at this top part of the clock.

'In the Land of Moon-Dial; that is where the challenge completes. On completion of the Challenge all hope is restored and you can return to your home-land. All parts of the challenge must be completed successfully for you to get home Jamie.'

The Time-Keeper was able to see my astonishment and how dazed I was.

She added, 'Now Jamie, I shall show you something to make your understanding clearer.'

The Clock outline vanished and the Time-Keeper raised her other hand in the air. I could see the engraved words *GNOBLE* that were on the outside of the clock. I knew it was the outside of the Grandfather's Clock immediately as you could see the letters engraved on the twirls of wood. What happened next almost blew me away. The Time-keeper started to wave her same hand in circles and the words got mixed up in sparkling glitter. When they returned together the letters from the outside clock started to change colour to a bright gold and moved places. The words then got re-arranged from back to front and came together to spell out:

'*Enchanted Land of BONG.*'

GNOBLE was not a name; it was an Enchanted Land. I swallowed in disbelief as my eyes looked like the big eyed bull-frog.

My eyes then flicked to the Time-Keeper as she started to talk to me in a courtly manner,

'Jamie, I am unable to be with you in person throughout this challenge but my presence will never leave you; I am with you always. I promise to be with you not only at those times of your journey when I know you need my help but during those times when you are successful.'

She then added, 'I will not be physically present but I promise you that at all times during your journey; I will be with you and to encourage the wisdom as a child you already have.'

She then nodded her head forwards as a courtesy and said,

'I am here to serve you.'

Chapter 6 - The Dark Hooded Stranger

As the guests left the marquee they walked outside over the fields of green into the Grand Hall. The weather outside seemed to be much cooler. I saw the Time-Keeper turn to Gem-Star and the Watcher on the grasslands and they both started to nod their heads in agreement with something, they looked as if they were arranging something. Gem-Star saw that I was watching and after she bowed before the Time-Keeper she then walked over towards me and smiled.

She told me, 'Dearest Chosen One, from another glorious home land. Thank you for coming to save us and I will welcome you on your journey to Our Land of Moon-Dial. My sisters would love to meet you dearest Chosen Guest.'

'I feel rather special being called Chosen One and Guest all the time,' I proudly said.

Gem-Star continued, 'My sisters look out to other universes using their enchanted golden telescopes. They would love to show you how they ensure all planets are in harmony and perfectly balanced.'

I smiled a terrific big smile showing her my white pearl coloured teeth.

'Wow, I have always wanted to use a telescope,' I declared.

She replied, 'Well when you come to the Land of Moon Dial we will ensure you experience enchanted telescopes in a very different way. But now there is something I must pass onto you prior to you starting the Challenge of Chime.'

As I stood before Gem-Star her hair was now a beautiful pale sparkling blue. She pulled from her pocket a little black sack and handed it to me.

'In this purse are special magical gems from our Land. These gems were a gift to my family. In fact they were given to my family as a thank you gift. From a truly wonderful character. That character once said I would know the time to pass them onto another being not from our home land. That time is now Jamie. These gems must be given to you.'

'Gosh,' I was dumb-struck. 'Pardon me Gem-Star but I am only ten years old. I have never been given gems as a present before. Usually it is a fishing rod, a cricket bat or even a ticket to see Spiderman. Are you sure these gems are for me? I checked.

Gem-Star was now a beautiful topaz orange colour with her hair gleaming like gold,

'The loving character I mention to you Jamie banished the Time-Taker some time ago from our home lands. My family received the gifts because during that time and after we promised to keep a look-out for the enemy and his return. We believe that all possibility exists with these gems being given to us Jamie. In any impossible situation. We know that our friend who gave them to us will one day know we have passed these gem stones on as we were meant to.'

Confused (this Gem-Star reminded me so much of my Aunt Jane it was spooky!) I asked,

'So are you saying Gem-Star that your friend knew I was coming here for you to give me these precious gem stones?'

Gem-Star smiled with her outfit floating in the gentle breeze outside.

'Of course our friend knew you were coming Jamie. He knows all that will be.'

As we continued to walk slowly Gem-Star then added,

'We kept the old ways of our Land of Bong true and alive in the most testing of times. Our friend crowned the Time-Keeper our ruler over the Land of Bong and we received the precious gems with the promise to one day pass them on.

'Who is this friend?' I said quite daunted.

'The Time-Keeper will share that with you at the appointed time Jamie. You must be patient and although want to know that now you must understand some things are not always best to know about straight away. Timing is important.'

Gem-Star who was now a glowing peach colour explained,

'Jamie, I was taught that at the right time I must be prepared to let go of something precious to receive something much greater in return.'

We walked together across the field as Gem-Star continued,

'Gems may be beautiful and precious Jamie but that is only if we are still able to exist in our home land to appreciate them.'

I got that and understood what Gem-Star meant.

She continued on, 'Jamie these gem stones have great power and are no simple jewels. I inform you that they have the greatest love poured into them containing: victory, strength, determination, courage and faith. At the right time you may use these jewels to help you with the Challenge of Chime. You will know when you are meant to use them and always remember this. The true glory lies in not keeping precious treasures to you but by sharing that glory with others.'

By the end of this discussion Gem-Star had turned into a beautiful glowing red ruby coloured outfit with hair to match.

'Thank you Gem-Star for helping me, I glowed in the twinkles of her dress.'

And soon enough we approached the entrance to the Grand-Hall Palace. Gem-Star left me and the Time-Keeper took me inside the Palace to her golden chair where I stood beside her as she seated herself. It was so full of spectacular dressed guests you could not see any of its beauty anymore. It was packed like a tin of sardines.

There was lots of hustle and bustle until the Time-Keeper raised her hand. She stood in silence and everyone else quickly followed and stopped their conversations as she stood.

'Friends of our home land the Enchanted Land of Bong. It is now time to position ourselves in preparation for the challenge ahead. You all know that the weather and air is colder now and you understand what this means. It is time for you all to take your places. I hold you to account for each task that is set in your land for Jamie. I account for each of you to use your gifts and knowledge with the wisdom of our ways that is yours. I honour each of you. Now be gone!'

In that one word 'Gone' each and every guest vanished out of the Great Hall. There was only the Time-Keeper and I left. It was so quiet and cold.

'It is time for us to move you onwards now Jamie; the moon-dial has risen and we are against time now. I must prepare you for your journey ahead. You will start the Challenge of Chime at the Staircase of Memories. You must ensure Jamie that you do not miss any of the steps out in this task. Often one prefers to jump and to skip a few steps when it comes to memories. In this case that would be dreadful.'

'Dreadful?' I queried.

'The stairs are magical. One would look at the staircase and think there are more stairs than there actually is. If you miss a step then you do not learn from the Staircase of Memories those valuable lessons that will benefit you. You may go through some steps quicker than others but not all of them. You will know what to do at the right time,' she explained.

I was listening to every precious word of advice that the Time-Keeper was prepared to give me. She dazzled in her gown whenever she moved. She walked with me towards glass-stained windows. I then asked her in a croaky voice,

'Is there anything else I must do Time-Keeper?'

'Yes Jamie. You must ensure that you move forwards up the Staircase of Memories. If you have something delightful that you may experience then yes do enjoy that moment but do not be fooled by staying still. You must keep yourself present in the moment and climb those stairs or you will not progress to get to the next Challenge.'

Just before we got to the entrance of a glass hallway that was small with an incredibly wide glass spiral staircase an enormous gust of wind blew open two of the large wooden doors. Clusters of fog followed through the opened doors. The fog grew taller from the ground and when it cleared there was a dark hooded cloaked stranger standing at the door entrance. You could not see any face inside the black hood as it was so large it would have covered any eyes or nose. All I could see from where I was standing was a red rose on his cloak and one hood filled with darkness. I kept feeling cold and numb. I did not want to move anywhere.

The Time-Keeper just gently nudged me through the entrance towards the glass staircase.

'You must keep out of sight now Jamie and start to climb the stairs. Go on now, quickly, there is no time to lose,' she whispered in my ear.

I am unsure if the hooded stranger saw my exit into the hallway but as I walked towards the stairs I could hear the words that passed between the Time-keeper and the hooded stranger.

I could hear the Time-Keeper speaking,

'As anticipated Time-Taker, we engage your presence once more after the Twist of our Key. We only ask you to abide by our ancient ways and to ensure that the 'Challenge of Chime' can progress according to the Enchanted Land of Bong's traditional way.'

I froze at the bottom of the stair case as I heard the cloaked Time-Taker speak. His voice so cold and stern it made me shiver inside. The fact that the Time-Taker was called a Time-Taker made me realise he was not a friendly character or guest I would like to see again.

'Come now, come now you glorious Time-Keeper. Do not so soon try to control me; I have only just arrived here in this enchanted land and regardless of the fact that you wear the Crown of Cogs you know I am the most powerful. I am not fooled by your charm Time-Keeper and I know the ancient old ways; my history created them.'

The Time-Taker fiddled with some beads he had around his neck that scooped down. On the end of these beds he had some type of clock-watch? It appeared to have numbers going backwards on it? And it appeared to be faceless with no dial to indicate the time? It was quite large to see it from where I was standing. The red rose he had in his cloak appeared to have petals dropping off it.

The Time-Keeper replied in an even softer tone,

'Time-Taker you may have created a part of the ancient old ways but by no means does it determine what we choose to do today in the moment or the present. Nor does it mean that your wicked attempts shall impact our everlasting future. Do not misunderstand my manner towards you Time-Taker. The Crown of Cogs symbolises the principles and values I display towards you and all others. Integrity may appear as charm to you but one greater than us all knows my intentions are clear in serving others.'

The Time-Taker replied, 'The great one you speak of has allowed me to enter this Land. If one was so great and wonderful, why would that be possible? Don't answer that Time-Keeper because I have the best plot that must be followed through. My plans are so outstanding that I cannot delay. I would not want to deny my great reputation in your Land and trust me when I say; I will ensure the Challenge of Chime is unsuccessful without doubt. There will be no more Enchanted Land of Bong; I will ensure that this boy without any doubt will fail his mission.'

Chapter 7 - Staircase of Memories

It was at that point I started to head towards the crystal glass staircase. Looking at the Staircase of Memories helped to distract me only for a few moments. I no longer could hear the voices but my thoughts were jumping around in my mind. I knew my hunch was right. That awkward strange feeling inside myself that the Time-Taker knew I was in the Land of Bong stirred inside my belly. He must have seen my exit to the glass hallway. I needed to move onwards as soon as possible. The whole challenge ahead of me was quite fascinating. As I already told you, I am a young boy inside an enchanted land. But I will say this to you. The Time-Taker looked very scary indeed. No face, just darkness inside his hood and coldness all around him.

'I hope I will not be seeing too much of him,' I whispered.

I was curious. I will admit that to you mainly about what the history was between the Time-Keeper and the Time-Taker. By the sounds of their brief talk I overheard they are certainly not friends. I am quite sure that the history between them both would be a great story for another book.

The shining glass stairway went around in a looped spiral and each time I climbed memories from my past flashed into my mind. It was a little bit like before when I touched the wooden panels but I really experienced these past moments as though I was back in time. I decided as I climbed to go as quickly up the staircase as possible so that I would not focus too much on the memories as the Time-Keeper had advised me to do so. 'I must try my best to not get stuck on here,' I recalled as I jumped up the stairs.

The memories flashed back to me starting with my first day at school to my favourite sweetshop. The favourite sweetshop memory was a little bit of a problem. Quite tricky as I could see the selection of ten-pence pick and mix sweet-bags before my eyes. Delicious sherbet fountains with liquorice fountains were placed next to sherbet dip-dabs. All of these were right there in front of me on a shelf. I could touch them packets and see behind them to where there were lots of white chocolate mice and white chocolate fish and chips in clear tubs. I loved that sweetshop and did not want to step up but I forced my right leg to move me onwards or I knew I would be in trouble.

I jumped quickly through the next step which was my birthday party. It was my 5th birthday because I jumped right through my Spiderman cake with candles in it. The next step took me to when I visited Emily after she had been born in the hospital. Now the next step was a struggle.

My Dad and I were spending time together fishing. He was making me laugh as he dropped a box of maggots all over the fishing bag by accident. 'Wow, this was one of the best days ever,' I smiled watching my Dad laughing so much he had tears in his eyes.

That was a great day and I really did not want to leave it. I stepped up onto my left leg and entered my own perfect heaven. I was in the music shop at Tottenham Court Road playing on a drum kit. I played those drums for real and it was awesome. I sounded so fantastic and I could see the shopkeeper's impressed face a young boy like me showing such talent for the drums.

'Bam, bam, bam,' I really used those drum sticks well. I didn't want to stop the flow of my music. Somehow I moved myself from the drum stool and stepped up the glass stairs again. My heart felt so happy playing music with those drums I could easily have continued on and on. Stuck forever in my own music.

The next step was my Head Teacher at school calling me out of the assembly seats to receive an award for my science project. I loved that day I was so pleased to have my work noticed by everyone. The next step was my marvellous worm farm. It was such good fun but not as much as the drum kit so I soon jumped to the next step.

I was baking with Aunt Jane. We made butterfly cakes and chocolate cornflake cakes. I was smothered in chocolate and Aunt Jane's kitchen was full of cakes everywhere.

I lifted up my foot and stepped into masses of muddy water. Now I was wearing wellington boots. I was jumping in massive puddle. I was outside in our huge garden getting soaked in the wet splashes. I was having a great time but I managed to keep moving and went forwards.

I stepped up on the glass staircase and entered the Scout's tent.

'ARGH!'

Straight into a battle with pillows. I was away with the pillow fun-fight with my fellow Scouts. Knowing this could go on for some time I stepped my left foot up and entered Christmas morning at home. Snow was outside the windows in the lounge and each window was decorated with fairy lights. Lots of wrapping paper was scrunched up over the carpets and new toys were all over the place.

I stepped my right foot up and was on an Easter Egg Hunt with Emily. We had found at least ten eggs between us and we only needed two more. I so wanted to get those last two eggs. I did not want to leave the egg hunt (it is my favourite time of year) but I knew I must step up quickly before I allowed myself to get into the game any further. Up the staircase again,

'This is not easy Time-Keeper,' I breathed in hoping that she would hear me from wherever she was right now.

This time I entered our library at home. I could hear my parents talking about how proud they were of me in the nativity play at school. How I had played the part of Joseph incredibly well and never forgot any of my lines. I wanted to hear more but I stepped up again because I knew when I was little how special that moment was to me. I felt so proud of my performance I wanted to receive the good comments from my parents again and again.

Now I was on the beach front throwing shells into the sea out of my bucket. I was keen to start my sand castle and to make it as huge as possible but I knew I must step up my right foot. I had to continue upwards. Next step, I had got twenty out of twenty in my spellings test at school and the classroom was clapping for my achievement.

I stepped up again. I had gone to a fancy dress party as Captain Hook and won the best Pirate costume prize. I was six years old. I had my own eye patch on with the most super sword. I stepped up again. I was climbing trees in the garden. I was swinging now from a tree branch in the sunshine and enjoyed the outdoors.

'I love this feeling,' I laughed. In that moment I stepped up again.

Then the next step took me back to an upsetting situation. I had broken a glass pane window in our green-house. Glass had gone all over our tomato plants. My mother was telling me off and I was stood in front of her as she waved her finger at me, yelling that I was irresponsible and must take more care. I must not ever do that again. At this point I really wanted to go back down the steps to the tree climbing event as it was guaranteed fun. The stone I threw at the bottle on the dustbin had totally missed the bottle and smashed into the green-house window. I could not move anywhere right now. I was a poor shot. I really felt frustrated by my mother as she did not realise I was just having fun outside. Usually I never miss the bottle shot and knock it straight over. I nodded my head in agreement with my furious Mother. Then somehow I managed to step up again instead of stepping down.

The next step was even more dreadful than the greenhouse memory. There I was lost in the middle of a family outing in Hyde Park, London. I was worried as our family had been walking by the Serpentine Lake (Aunt Jane has been swimming in this lake before) and picked the perfect spot for our picnic. We had gone for a family day out and walked for some time around the lake.

When I turned to sit down for our picnic all of the family had disappeared! Not one of them was with me. All of the family had gone out of my sight. I must have been about five years of age. There I was again, in the moment standing next to the Serpentine Lake on my own feeling so scared. My nerves were like a prickly hedgehog and I could not find anyone to help me. I could not step up the staircase. I was too busy looking around for my family again feeling that same panic I felt when a child is lost. Then out of the blue almost like someone had opened up my brain and posted me the thought I remembered something so important.

'I do find my family in the end. They were behind that lot of green trees and bushes not too far away.'

I started to talk to myself, 'Jamie, you must not worry. You find everybody in the end and it all works out well. Do not panic!' Suddenly I focused on where I needed to be. 'To keep climbing,' I remembered as I moved myself up the stairs and progressed onto the next glass step.

Suddenly I was at school and it our Sport's day. This was one of my most terrible days. I did not like this at all but I knew how bad the last few steps were and could not face climbing down the stairs. At school all of our classes were grouped and picked for teams by two boys. Two boys I really did not care for in the slightest. Elliott and Jake were often unkind to other children and very cheeky to adults in front of them and when they turned their backs. Today they were both picking their team players and I was left on the field as the last player to be selected. Might I add that they did this because I did not try to fit in with them or please them like other friends did.

I was standing there out on the field waiting for them to call my name and both boys sniggered at each other and did not call my name out. I could feel my face getting red beneath my freckles and sheer awkwardness filled me from top to toe. Eventually Mr Richards our teacher realised the boys were being unkind yet again and called my name to put me into Jake's team. I could feel my cheeks blushing and tears in the back of my eyes as I lifted my foot up to climb onto the next step.

Then there were no more memories to be seen. I must have climbed around the crystal staircase as when I looked around me there were no more memories to be seen. There were no more stairs to climb. I looked behind and I could see that I was at the top of the spiral staircase.

I could feel a breeze in the air whipping past and around me and as I walked forwards onto the crystal flooring the wind became stronger, harder and faster. Suddenly all I could hear was a loud voice singing and as the wind became stronger the voice became stronger. The last thing I heard before everything became dark was, 'Mooooooove out of the way!'

Chapter 8 - Mr and Mrs Pendulum

I could feel the breeze over my face and a discussion going on above me as I tried to open my eyes.

'Mr Bob when do you think he will wake up?' asked the female voice.

'Mrs Lyre I think it may be that he is waking up now. Do you think we should go a bit faster to get more wind on to his face to fan him?'

'That is a most splendid, splendid idea my Mr Bob, not too fast though as we must keep things to time.'

Fast wind blew onto my face as I could hear a whipping sound above me. I opened my eyes and I could see two huge golden discs above my head swinging in opposite directions to each other. As they passed each other I could hear them speaking to each other? I realised these two discs were hanging quite low from some high place so I rolled away from the crystal staircase to the opposite direction. Perhaps I could possibly manage to stand without getting myself knocked over.

'A wee bit slower now Mr Bob as our guest has awoken, we do not need to keep this speed up anymore. What a splendid idea that was,' said one of the golden discs to the other.

As I stood in the corner I gasped when I noticed that each of these huge golden discs had faces with eyes, eyelashes and mouths. One of them with the male voice had a droopy moustache.

'Greetings our guest Jamie, it is a pleasure to receive you in our Land of Pendulum,' said the male golden disc. 'Let me introduce us both to you,' he said as he kept swinging from side to side making me feel quite dizzy.

My name is Bob Pendulum and this is my wife Lyre Pendulum and we have been waiting for you. Are you alright Mr Jamie? I hope we did not injure you when you fell down?'

I found this all quite fascinating how conversation took place as the Pendulums swooped just to the right height to speak to me and then whizzed past me and each other up into the air. Both Pendulums were going in different directions and took it turns to speak to me. I must say it was quite a spectacular sight.

Mrs Pendulum started to speak, 'You really are a great boy Jamie and it is so splendid to see you inside our Land of Bong but we do not have time to waste.' Then Mr Pendulum added as he was swinging past me, 'That is correct, you must progress onto the next task and that means seizing the opportunity to climb upwards.' I questioned Mr and Mrs Pendulum, 'Thank you for helping me, but I am not quite sure I understand what you mean? What does that mean about seizing the opportunity to move upwards? I looked around the room and I could see no other exit points apart from the crystal staircase entrance. The same entrance that I had climbed to reach this exact place.

Mrs Pendulum spoke, 'My dear we are unable to tell you what you must do exactly. We are only able to inform you that you must seize the opportunity to climb upwards.'

Both Mr and Mrs Pendulum kept crossing each other by as I kept thinking to myself how I could move upwards. There was nowhere else in the room I could exit.

I said, 'How will that be possible?' as I looked around the room they both kept swinging past me.

'There is no time to waste Jamie,' said Mr Pendulum, 'You must leave in a few minutes or you will not get to the next task.

'At that time I had moved so that Mr and Mrs Pendulum were facing me directly and I could see that there was a moment when they both crossed over and were just above my height. Then I got an idea.

'Mr and Mrs Pendulum, I hope you will excuse me but I think I need your help and that means using you both to climb upwards?'

Mrs Pendulum got very delighted at this stage and her golden cheeks got quite pink, 'Splendid Jamie! Well done. Just tell us exactly how and what you want to do.'

Mr Pendulum then added, 'We are unable to tell you what to do Jamie, you must follow your instincts and do whatever to complete your task.'

I knew I had to move fast. For a few turns I watched as Mr and Mrs Pendulum passed by me they were just above my level. I held up my arms and I could see that I would be able to grab one of them that whizzed past me. I looked upwards and I could see a hole in the roof top that would get me out onto the next floor.

'Possibly onto the next challenge?' I whispered,

'No time to loose.' I started to count,

'One, two and three. One, two and THREE. ONE, TWO AND THREE!'

I jumped on the three with my arms up in the air just at the right moment. As I jumped with arms up right into the air, I grabbed hold of the rim of Mr Pendulum's chin. Now here I was swinging in the wind up and down. I tried desperately to grab hold of Mr Pendulum's moustache. As I did amazingly out of nowhere an invisible staircase became visible and golden over Mr Pendulum's face. During this time both Mr and Mrs Pendulum had stopped speaking to me. Had their magical powers stopped? Both of their eyes were closed and although you could see the outline of their faces they never spoke a word. The golden ladder was becoming more obvious now.

As the wind brushed against my body I kept my face and body as tight to the staircase as possible so that I could climb faster. All of those trees I climbed must have prepared me for this challenge I thought. It was quite a task especially as I went through the air from side to side. Up to the right I went. High into the air and then down I swooped. Up, high in the air to the left. Then swooping downwards again; down and to the right and upwards.

If you find reading that part of my story tricky I do apologise. It cannot be as bad reading it as doing it. This was worse and much higher and scary than the roller-coaster I had experienced at Alton Towers or any of the rides at Light-water Valley. I just kept on climbing upwards keeping my face towards the ladder in the wind. To make it easier I tried to move up the steps when Mr and Mrs Pendulum crossed each other at a lower level. Soon I was feeling less of a breeze as I had climbed passed Mr

Pendulum's face and I was much higher in the air. Quite close to the opened roof-top. Now I had passed onto a skinny pure golden staircase that led me up through an open cavity in the ceiling. Just as I climbed through the cavity into a new place I heard Mrs Pendulum call out,

'Splendid Jamie! Now whatever you do just make sure you don't waste too much time on the next task.'

Once again the Pendulums were chatting to each other again and their magic had returned.

Chapter 9 - Loosing Track of Time

The Time-Taker from another Land watched Jamie though a magical misty cloud he had directly in front of him. The Time-Taker observed as he watched Jamie climb through the cavity towards the next Challenge of Chime and he could feel his own annoyance growing. The red rose he wore on the front of his hooded gown lost a petal onto the dusty ground he stood on.

The Time-Taker snivelled,

'The Challenge has started and my time is not as long as I would like it to be therefore I will cause as much turmoil as I can; while I can. This boy is smart and he is bold,' he muttered to himself.

'Perhaps it is time to create a distraction so that he is unable to keep his focus from his true purpose. I shall cause him to be so stirred up and wrapped up in a situation he is unable to concentrate on anything other than the trouble and frustration I cause.'

The Time-Taker smiled to himself as he waved his hand and finger towards the cloud of smoke. As the cloud vanished the Time-Taker declared,

'It is time for things to get just a bit more heavy and pressured for you my unwanted guest Jamie.'

***

'Whoa!' I rolled over onto the paved floor from the golden ladder and kept as low as I possibly could. There were lots of heavy golden lanterns hanging above my head.

'I would not like to get knocked out again,' I stated as I lay flat on my belly. When I turned over I suddenly realised that right at the very top of the golden lanterns were those strange characters. The ones from the marquee tent who wore suits created out of watches.

'TOOD-A-LOO,' one of the Watchers roared jumping in the air from one of the golden lanterns onto another as it went downwards.

Lying on the floor I just watched this incredible act like something out of the circus it was totally amazing. 'TOOD-A-LOO,' a different watcher repeated as she dived downwards from another lantern going upwards to then another lantern that started to moved downwards.

'Wow!' I was astonished.

What fun as well as dangerous this diving act seemed to me as I just observed. From one lantern to another lantern the Watchers jumped shouting out to each other just before they dived. What was quite distinct is the way the Watchers put goggles on before they dived and jumped onto another Lantern.

'WOW!' I shouted, 'What a job that must be!'

As I sat on the floor watching this magnificent act and hearing the Watchers cry out,

'TOOD-A-LOO' about every ten seconds (the full diving act with goggles was quite a perfectly timed performance) I called out at the top of my voice,

'Hello there, I am here Mr Watcher. How do you do Sir?'

The Watcher (that is what the Time-Keeper called these folks did she not?) waved his arm and then all of the others alike him on top of the golden lanterns waved. All of a sudden they started to jump from one golden lantern onto another high up in the air.

'TOOD-A-LOO, TOOD-A-LOO' MOVE IT DOWN OUR GUEST HAS ARRIVED. Welcome to the Land of Weights!' he yelled.

As they all jumped onto one golden lantern they lowered down towards me on top of it. I was quite surprised at how many Watchers could fit on top of one golden lantern. It took great skill and technique. At a certain point they all jumped off and the lantern moved back on itself upwards. I was surrounded by lots and lots of watchers. Some were female and some were male wearing multi-coloured outfits with different shaped watches all over them. Their clothing outfits looked like jigsaw puzzles all joined together out of watches. They fitted together to make perfect bright clothing. 'How bizarre!' I stammered.

Quite a few of these bright cheeked characters had watches wrapped around their heads with the clock-face on the front of their fore-heads. On top of the clock-face or on top of the Watcher's head there was a pair of very brightly coloured goggles.

'That is a most unusual place to be wearing a watch,' I enquired.

The colours were bursting throughout these outfits in green, blue, and yellow. What a great fashion unlike my boring clothes I thought.

'It is very wonderful to have you in our Land Mr Jamie,' stated the Watcher as he shook my hand.

I took the Watcher's hand delighted to be meeting him in person and I shook it a few times.

'How do you do Mr Watcher, I am Jamie your special guest.'

The Watcher beamed at me, 'Call me Mr Watcher if you prefer. Welcome. You are now in the Land of Weights.'

Before I could ask about the next Challenge of Chime all I could hear was

'Look out everyone' followed by

'STAND BACK!' We all stood back as the massive golden lanterns a total of three landed with a huge thud onto the ground in front of us. The floor we stood on vibrated and we all got a shock from that.

'Just as well my team of Watcher's watch over this place all the time isn't it Jamie?' Mr Watcher pointed out.

He stepped forwards and walked around. He did not look as shocked as the rest of us by the lanterns crashing down.

'We could have been hurt badly!' I uttered to one of the female watchers who nodded her head in agreement with me.

By gum it was fortunate that we had taken those steps back quickly or anyone of us would have been splattered as none of the golden lanterns were light and delicate. They were heavy! The Watcher turned to his family and spoke in a calming tone,

'This interruption is the Time-Taker's works and it is corruption at his hands. I say it is interruption as we all know the next challenge cannot be completed without our golden weights and balance keeping everything to time. Time is being lost right now!' The Watcher added, 'Jamie if we are not to time, you cannot progress onto the next challenge.'

I gently spoke, 'If you don't mind me asking Mr Watcher. I thought that those three large things that landed were golden lanterns?'

Mr Watcher smiled, 'No my dearest Mr Jamie, they are not golden lanterns. In fact, they are golden weights that ensure we have balance and perfect time across all of our Lands including your home land Jamie.

A female Watcher continued on the explanation,

'Watchers are responsible to ensure that we have perfect balance of the weights in order to keep time. Most of our time is taken by our Watchers moving across our weights to and from to ensure that they are at the correct height, correct balance to influence the correct time. That is apart from when the clock strikes on the hour. We must ensure our Weights are TOTALLY (yes she did shout out TOTALLY very loudly!)

perfect in co-ordination. We use our watches to ensure to the very second that all goes to time. We use a method called 'synchronisation,' she smiled.

'I see, so they are weights and not lanterns,' I commented.

'Exactly,' said another male Watcher with very red cheeks, 'The problem we have now is that the weights have all stopped still and that must mean that someone has meddled with the cable pulleys that we use to operate them. Thank goodness we had all climbed off to meet you Mr Jamie or we would have been in big trouble if not squashed to the ground!'

For some time we stood looking at the golden weights and the twisted cables that appeared to be loose from the higher ground that held them up in place tightly. Mr Watcher spoke again,

'Jamie, you must complete the Challenge of Chime in our land but before that can be accomplished our golden weights must be fully functioning. We cannot be standing around anymore wasting time. You must provide a solution and fast so that you can progress onto the next quest.

All eyes of the Watchers were on me. They seemed very dependent on me coming up with the solution. I was red in my face as I thought hard about what I could do to get the cable pulleys and the cables sorted out so that the Weights would be functioning again. What a task. I kept thinking to myself and I walked away in private. How could any of us get to such heights to tie the cables back up was truly frustrating me.

'I need help!' I declared.

All went quiet around me. The Watchers for the first time went silent and ever so clearly I heard a female soft voice saying,

'All of the resources you need are already within you Jamie.'

That was it. I walked back and forth and then I answered the voice,

'I would need a pair of wings to get this job done myself and I don't have wings!'

Then I got it. I really got it. It came to me in a flash of inspiration. Real genius as I did not have wings to get the job done but I knew someone who did. Orange's feather got pulled out of my pocket and I raised it into the air to signal her. The Watcher said,

'Jamie what are you doing with that old Plumage feather?'

Another old grey-haired Watcher said,

'Look at that he is waving it about in the air, like a signal? I think he is calling someone?'

In less than a few moments Orange flew into the higher land and she was swooping around with her wings fully spread out. She looked beautiful and from afar looked more like a large golden eagle spreading her huge wings. From a great height Orange made a dive downwards towards us on the lower ground. In no time she was stood in front of me and her wings were down as she spoke,

'O' Chosen one. I am here to oblige, how can I serve you?'

It did not take me long to explain to Orange how she needed to fly high up and ensure that the cables were tied so that the heavy weights were not loose on the lower ground but able to hang. The plan was to tie the cable pulleys so that the weights could balance as usual with the Watchers on top of them.

As I shared this with Orange she flew up onto the weights and checked that the cables were fastened securely through the cable pulleys.

'O' Chosen One, I believe it must be from higher Land that the cables have been cut down or released. I shall fly up to that higher Land with the three cables and ensure that they are re-joined and fixed. This action will ensure that our time can be precise and the weights rebalanced at the earliest opportunity.'

The Watchers helped Orange by giving her the cables to carry with her additional legs or arms. Soon Orange had her wings fully flexed and she swooped and swooped until she was quite out of sight. During this time we waited and all was silent as we knew that the Time-Taker had started to distract my tasks.

The Watchers were becoming quite disturbed and started to argue and get overly disgruntled with each other. According to the mature Watchers that were quite old and wise this was quite ordinary. The younger Watchers needed much structure and a demanding routine to keep them focused. One old Watcher explained,

'If they do not have a disciplined purpose and duty their behaviour causes havoc.'

This was quite worrying news to me and I hoped that my favourite Plumage and friend Orange would hook up our cables fast. Fast so that the Watchers could also get back to their work on the weights screaming 'Tood-a-loo' as soon as possible.

Then it happened. One of the golden weights started to move upwards into the air. Then another of the golden weights started to move upwards into the air. Then the last golden weight moved up into the air. The cable pulleys were being pulled by Orange who was totally out of sight. The second golden weight was just slightly higher than the other two. The Watchers were overjoyed and as they started to move into the air as they all hopped onto the golden weights and immediately stared at each other's watches and their own watches.

All I could hear as Watchers were going into the air was,

'Keep to Time. Please do keep to time.'

No sooner than the weights were in the air the Watchers started off again jumping from one weight to another weight making the weights alter heights yet again. Orange did not return to see me but she did fulfil her promise. I started to get nervous as I became aware of how much time had gone by with the frustration of the cables being released.

I announced,

'That Time-Taker really did mean business and meant what he said about wanting me to fail.'

I was in deep thought about the next task when the flooring beneath me started to move. I didn't have time to shout, scream or to move. I fell to the ground. I could see the paved flooring shuffle up and down. Then it folded up and over. Suddenly I was enclosed in a room of paved golden tiles that were originally on the ground!

I stayed on the ground speechless. Then a mouth formed out of the golden paving. It was a massive mouth in front of me and it appeared to be wearing cubed-lipstick.

'Oh-Oh,' I uttered. 'What's happening now?'

The mouth opened and wailed, 'What's happening now? What's happening now? You need to be patient and wait for ME to tell you what is happening now!'

'Oh, I'm sorry,' I babbled not having a clue how to handle this Mouth.

'So!' The Mouth rambled. 'Ahem. Would you like me to tell you what is happening now?'

'Yes please!' I whimpered.

'You must solve this puzzle now and if you are successful you will return to where I collected you from below the golden weights. Just remember this. Not everything that looks good tastes good,' the Mouth announced.

I never said a word and just waited.

The Mouth started to hum and when it first opened ridiculous items came out of the huge hole in its mouth. First there was a random fish playing a piano, then a flying horse. Then a cream cake that had running legs. Followed by words in cubes that read,

'CAN, YOU, PLACE, THE, CUBES, TO, BUILD, A, STRONG, CHARACTER, WHO, WILL, GET, YOU, OUT, OF, HERE?'

The words in cubes were in the air dangling and I replied,

'Yes, I can.'

The Mouth started to hum again and opened this time with lots of different cooking ingredients flying out towards me: flour, raisins, brandy, mixed peel, eggs, butter, mixed spice, nutty almonds, baking powder sugar and cake decorations. The items lingered in front of me and then by magic a huge mixing bowl appeared underneath the cubed items.

'Not everything that looks good tastes good?' I babbled.

Immediately I went straight to the cake decorations that were the most detailed and attractive sight. The decorations ranged from cherries, frosted sugar lemons and oranges to chocolate flowers.

'Yummy!' I gulped.

Of course you can imagine I wanted them in my huge bowl if not in my own mouth straight away. I was so lured by the cherries as they were bright red and looked like miniature toffee apples.

'I want these for certain because they look nice and a cake must look nice,' I uttered as I lifted my hand to select the cherries. Just as my fingertips got ready to touch the cherries I pulled back.

'It is impossible to make a cake to start with just with cake decorations. Even though they look gorgeous!' I blurted out. Followed by what I had learned from Aunt Jane, 'Some ingredients build our cake, others preserve it some just make it look appetising.'

I moved myself in front of the core ingredients for my cake and started to put them into the mixing bowl. In went the flour first with the sugar and eggs. A magical spoon appeared when I added ingredients into the bowl so I started to mix it together. I continued on and added in the butter and stirred followed by the baking powder. Just then stars started to leap out of the mixing bowl.

'Wait a minute! I have not finished yet!' I shouted.

The stars were floating up above the Mouth and I realised that on the stars words were written; honesty, trustworthy and appreciative. The last two stars read; disciplined and patient.

I decided to carry on. I added in the mixed spice, almonds, raisins and mixed peel to my mixing bowl and stirred it with the spoon. Then lastly I added the brandy.

'This smells good!' I commented.

'YIKES!' I shrieked as the stars above the Mouth dived back into my bowl and took out the rest of my cake mixture.

'HANG ON A MINUTE!' I complained to the Mouth. 'What's going on?'

Now all the stars were lined above the mouth.

Again words appeared written on the stars; generous, zealous, faithful, respectful and kind.

The only thing left untouched in the ingredients were the delicious looking cake decorations.

'BAM, BANG, BAM, BANG, BAM, BANG, BAM, BANG, BAM, BANG!'

I darted down to the ground as this noise sounded like a shot gun.

The cake decorations (including the bright red cherries) had changed into black stinky fumes and the smell was unbearable. I looked at the words inside the fumes that floated and they read; greed, hate, selfishness and despair.

My goodness I was so pleased I had picked the right ingredients and the magic had started before I had gone to decorate my cake with the fancy sugared lemons and oranges!

The Mouth opened wider and wider. The cubes overlapped making it much bigger inside. Then it swallowed all of my stars that flew out of my mixing bowl.

The Mouth then spoke,

'A cake of the wise reflects what is good 'O' Chosen one. A cake of the wise builds a magnificent character. It does not require outside appearances. The fanciest decorations do not build the foundations of a great cake not do they build a strong character.'

The decorations vanished. The Mouth started to shift again with cubes folding outwards and down. I lay on the floor too scared to move.

I could no longer see the Mouth. I was surrounded by cubes everywhere and then they started to fall to the ground. I closed my eyes and when I opened them the paved floor was still and had returned to normal.

I stood up. I walked around the weights and the light shone through the glass onto the golden weights. The brightness cast down onto me. I walked around the glass windows that surrounded the full square of the Land of Weights I walked on.

I looked into the glass that was shining and all I could see outside was multi-coloured patterns. The colours outside the glass looked familiar to me but before I could think where I had seen those colours before, something seemed to be spinning in front of me in the actual glass.

'What on earth is going on now?' I gasped.

I could see in the glass that it was cut at an angle. Not at ninety degrees (yes I did learn that at school) but less than that. It was very lovely the spinning colours as the light really did shimmer onto the glass. 'GOSH! Look at that!' I remarked.

There inside the spinning colours in the glass I saw the crowd of Smithereens that I met at the unusual event were now in the middle of these colours. They were inside the glass?

'Can you hear me?' I shouted.

No answer. In fact, right in front of me there in the glass was the sweet girl whose dress was made out of glass droplets; twirling around in front of me. She was adorable and I think she must have been the same age as Emily. She smiled at me and then nodded her head.

'So you can hear me!'

She nodded her head again. That was a good start.

Chapter 10 - The Mysterious Cave

How I had not managed to see these glass people before was beyond me. They lived in glass! How more weird could this Grandfather's Clock possibly be? How on earth did people manage to live in glass; how did they breathe? I know they were made of glass but the whole thing was rather bizarre. I saw the Smithereens (plenty of them to say the least) waving at me from inside the glass panel. They appeared to be waving their arms out in a spinning direction and then they were pointing at me. 'Are you asking me to spin around?' I asked demonstrating a spin towards the Smithereens.

At that point the Smithereens were nodding their heads at me. So indeed, I started to spin myself around immediately next to the glass panel, round and around I went. Faster and faster I went. All I could feel at this time was a squashed feeling. I suppose it is like when you try to cram in too much into your sandwich box for school. I felt like that and I tried to keep my eyes open but with such a sensation of being squashed and pulled at the same time. Believe me it was not possible to do so.

As soon as the feelings of being squashed left me I opened my eyes slowly to find that I was on the cool glass floor inside the glass panel surrounded by Smithereens. I looked through the glass and I could see the exact same place where I stood only moments before I started spinning. The Smithereens were a variety of crystal glass shapes and sizes but one thing they all had in common. They all had the same triangular shaped glass hats. I gasped as I saw how the Smithereens glided across the glass panel I was amazed. Smithereens in their home land did not walk. They glided as though they had ice-skates on.

'Gosh that is just such good FUN!' I admitted.

Believe me that they did not have ice-skates on such. Not as we do when ice-skating in England but you would have thought so. These folks were tall, medium and short and of all different ages. The older Smithereens appeared to have little cracks in the glass around their eyes or on their foreheads a bit like my Grandmother's wrinkles.

One very radiant Smithereen introduced herself.

'I am Shimmer of the Smithereens and very proud to meet you Jamie,' she said. She continued, 'We hoped you would continue to walk and realise that the next part of the Challenge is indeed in our home land.

'What is your home called?' I enquired.

'The Land of Bevelled Glass but you can call it the Land of Bevel,' Shimmer explained, 'It leads you onwards to your journey into the next Land. You have done incredibly well Jamie to find us. It could have taken you so much longer to realise this is where you needed to be. It must have been fun learning how to access our Land of Bevelled Glass. Spinning at high speed! At least Jamie, you are here now.'

I asked Shimmer, 'Are you the Queen of the Smithereens?' She certainly looked like a Queen with such a magnificent outfit of glass droplets and petticoats beneath made from frilly waves of glass. She responded,

'Jamie, I am not the Queen of the Land and what you will find throughout our Land is that the only difference between a true leader and her people is the responsibilities a leader holds.'

Shimmer smiled at me, she was quite bright to look at with all of the glass around her and she answered, 'All of us Smithereens are leaders, if we all didn't lead ourselves first in our duties and responsibilities we would not sustain the Land of Bevel.'

I asked the important question,

'Shimmer where is the next challenge in the Land of Bevel? I'm so worried about the time flying past and I must continue to do the tasks. I don't want us all to be in trouble.'

Shimmer responded, 'Jamie you are a noble gentleman and I shall now take you to the Bevel Glass Cave for your next task. All of us Smithereens give you much hope and encouragement. As a gift we will offer you this.'

At that point Shimmer passed me a scroll rolled up with a glass bow wrapped around it. She explained to me,

'The scroll is made of glass and it was created from our Bevel Glass Cave. It will open easily for you when it comes to you making your choices during the challenge Jamie. The challenge is inside the cave.'

'Choices I must make? I questioned.'

'Yes Jamie. The choices you must make. Everyone knows that one who wavers and lacks conviction in their decision-making is a weak character. Throughout the Challenge of Chime you will be faced with choices and responses that one day others will know of. Ultimately Jamie you must respond to the questions you are asked and be bold with them. Now then, to the Bevel Glass Cave we must go. Jamie we must not waste any more time.'

I walked whilst the Smithereens glided over the glass flooring for quite some time. During this journey the Smithereens gave me a glass with fluid and frosty ice-cubes in it. What was amazing about this drink is that it was bubbling and warm?

'Shimmer, what do you call this drink?' I asked.

She answered, 'The name of it is glass-boiled cordial. We drink it very hot but we know from a past experience that your kind from other worlds prefer it cooled down or it can born you,' she said.

'Born me?' I repeated. 'I think you mean burn me?' I added.

Shimmer expressed delight to be fully understood now as she smiled from ear to ear.

'That is right Jamie, it would BURN you. Unlike us Smithereens we are made of the finest glass that can tolerate such heat the drink is always extremely hot. We

Smithereens are created into our kind through such furnace but your kind is unable to take such heat.'

The cordial was delicious. It really did refresh me. The only way I can describe the taste is fizzy tutti-frutti flavoured or something quite like it.

***

From a distant land the Time-Taker was watching Jamie and the Smithereens glide over the glass land towards the Cave of Bevel through a misty cloud he had created.

'Hmm! I thought Jamie would have been foolish and try to go in an upwards direction during the Challenge of Chime. I thought he would follow his new found friends the Watchers. Those precious Watchers' and their precious, stupid weights. Argh! How did YOU so young access the Land of Bevelled Glass!'

The Time-taker was unimpressed how Jamie had used the tail feather of the Plumage to fix the cable.

'He thinks he can meddle with my tricks and delay tactics but not this time around,' the Time-Taker bragged full of suppressed anger.

He was furious that Jamie's distraction at the weights had not been for long enough and he kept muttering,

'I'll show him for getting into a Land of Bevel.' Enough of this he thought.

As he twisted himself around in front of the misty cloud in anger the petals fell onto the ground from his only red rose. As the Time-Taker watched a few petals fall he remembered a long, long time ago.

***

'I have brought you something from the garden as a gift,' the boy smiled.

He lifted up the red rose for her to take it from him and as she took the rose their hands touched.

'That is thoughtful and kind of you to think of me. Tell me why did you pick and bring me such a red rose today?' the pretty girl asked.

'I picked it because I miss you when we are not together,' he said.

***

The Time-Taker shook his head as he did not want to remember such thoughts. He stooped low in darkness hiding everything around him. Rose petals and grey smoke remained from the misty cloud as the Time-Taker vanished.

***

Soon Jamie and the Smithereens were at the entrance of the cave. There was readiness for the next task in the Challenge of Chime. Shimmer spoke,

'Jamie it is of great significance that you use the scroll and know that you are here at the Cave of Bevel because you are ready for this.'

I started to feel angst about going into the cave on my own,

'I am still at school Shimmer. Am I really old enough to go into this cave on my own and do this task?'

Shimmer touched my face with her hand; so smooth and very cold.

'In our Land Jamie the decisions a child makes throughout their life into young adulthood are so valuable. In fact, how you step up to the challenges life throws at you chisels your character like a perfect glass sculpture and all that you will become. Always remember Jamie it is not how old you are that is such a crucial matter when it comes to challenges in life. It is the decision to do what is right in all that is dark that matters.'

Then she questioned me, 'Jamie, how do you want to be remembered as a child?'

I responded, 'I would like to be remembered as one who had fun and treated people kindly. Who got the best spellings results in my class!'

Shimmer replied, 'Jamie, all achievements are good especially as you are growing and faced with so many opportunities to show your best. Remember this though Jamie. To have achievements is nothing without a true character. This task my friend will add to your soul regardless of the outcome. You cannot fail by trying.'

Shimmer hugged me, she felt incredibly cold and although it was a chilly hug I felt much happier and entered the Cave of Bevel with my glass scroll ready for the next challenge.

Inside the glittering cave it was so bright and there were glass iced-shapes all over the walls and over the roof of the cave. After walking for at least ten minutes into the cave I saw a lake full of bubbles. Out of it bubbles came up into the air and floated. When they reached the roof of the cave they absorbed into the roof and then a most beautiful shape would be created almost like a glass icicle. There were swirls and whirls and it reminded me of our Christmas decorations on the Christmas tree at home. The swirls and whirls of colour were blue with white and silver and they sparkled so lovely. Then what I saw next was quite spectacular. From up high a tiny ray of sunshine beamed through the cave through the smallest cavity; it was a tiny dot. At the point where it beamed there was an incredible hole melting in the glass that formed a slide going out of the cave downwards. Although the point of the beam in the cave roof was small the hole created at the end of the sun rays was actually quite huge.

I kept pacing around inside the cave until a voice echoed that said the following,

'You are in the Cave of Bevel and to leave this cave you must respond to each request otherwise you will remain here like many others.'

My stomach started to squelch and feel like a washing machine spinning around and around. I kept quiet. Then across the cave one of the cave walls lightened up in a bright whitish blue light. There inside I could see other creatures like animals still and with scared expressions on their faces. They looked like frozen sculptures trapped inside the wall. Now I really felt nervous and terrified. The light fell dark once more and the cave returned to its normal appearance hiding the frozen creatures.

'Visitor, Are you ready to answer my requests in our Cave of Bevel?' the voice enquired.

'I am ready,' I declared.

***

The Time-Taker was on the other side of the Cave of Bevel to the Smithereens and watching through the misty smoke that covered the cave walls. He could view exactly what was going on with Jamie. He could see everything and was enjoying the nervousness that Jamie experienced.

'I shall add some more anxiety and nerves to your experience Jamie. Fear is the greatest enemy of the mind. You shall have so much that you become stuck and incapable of going anywhere or doing anything,' he warned.

The Time-Taker laughed, 'Especially now you have met my frozen creatures!'

He stopped being spitefully happy with himself as he grabbed his beads and looked at his watch that did not go forwards and waved his arm to create another smoke screen. He could see into another Land.

The Time-Taker watched the Time-Keeper as she walked across her room to look out of her window. He could not believe how composed she was now that he had returned. He was on his own now and would never forgive her.

'You will be punished Time-Keeper. After all of this time I have waited patiently to punish you and you will never, ever reject me again,' he vowed.

He despised her vulnerability but more so her patience and kindness.

'If my plans work Time-Keeper my planet will never return and that is because I will be Ruler over the Land of Bong and own you with all other universes. He violently laughed.

'There will be no need for that planet to exist. Never! Ever! Again!'

The Time-Taker started to hunch downwards and then gradually raising his arms stood up tall. He raised his hands up to the glass sky and then waved them in a large circle quite a few times. As he did this the smoke filtered away and the land became very cold and icy.

***

Out of the ordinary Jamie suddenly started to panic. He felt very uneasy. He could feel goose-bumps and his nerves prickling throughout his body. He had never experienced such fear before and had no idea where such panic had come from.

The voice then spoke again,

'Are you ready for my first request Visitor?'

***

Outside, the Time-Taker smiled as he was now sensing how nervous and agitated Jamie was feeling. The Time-Taker took pleasure in chaos and creating fear in others.

Quite smug the Time-Taker sneered,

'Perhaps it is time for you to become like so many others who got in my way and be stuck forever and frozen.'

The Time-Taker watched Jamie.

'I enjoy the fact I can so easily control and create your fears Jamie!'

He caused Jamie to start walking backwards gradually without him even noticing that he was doing it.

'I think shortly you will be taking a slide to your doom Jamie,' the Time-Taker had a wicked laugh. He smiled to himself a very sly smile.

***

I really would like to leave this place right now, I thought. My whole body felt like I had spikes growing out of it. Rather uncomfortable! All I could do was think about how uncomfortable I felt and uneasy. I felt much worse than when I get ready to do my horrible science tests at school. Even more dreadful than when I'm told off by my parents for doing something wrong.

I started to say,

'No I am not ready in a quiet low voice,' when suddenly by magic something terrific occurred.

The glass bow on the glass scroll unfastened itself and the scroll started to open up.

Then 'Yes I am ready,' came out of my mouth without me trying to say it? I just said

'Yes' to the Voice followed by,

'Crumbs, how did that happen?'

I had never felt so uncertain in all of my time in the Grandfather's Clock. This moment was scary! At school I never felt so scared and stuck like this. Being stuck in the mud is quite like how I felt. Flummoxed is the word Aunt Jane would use.

Before I had time to dwell on myself or my feelings any further as Dad would say 'like a wild rabbit in the car headlights,' I was distracted. One of the large silver crystal glass bubbles came out of the boiling pool towards me. It didn't go up towards the ceiling this occasion to form a new icicle.

It just gracefully moved over so that it was positioned just above my head and then dark blue curly writing appeared inside the bubble. The writing said,

'What gift is given to all in your world today and tomorrow?

It is given freely for you to use?'

My goodness I thought. I started to think and ponder. Now how curious is this. On the glass scroll I was holding from the Smithereens a picture appeared and it was like a moving picture. The moving picture was of me playing the drums at my friend's house. I was thumping the drums and slamming the symbols. That picture then disappeared. All different thoughts went through my mind from being musical, to having fun and making people happy. Then something came to me and I have no idea of where it came from but I stuttered,

'Talent?'

Suddenly the crystal bubble went up to the roof top and formed another icicle and a new sparkling glass bubble came out of the rippling pool towards me. This one was bright white. Again on the glass bubble was some dark blue curly writing. It said,

'What poison in your world is an invisible poison to all mankind?'

Now this was really a tricky one.

'Invisible poison? I have never heard of such a poison? Does this really exist?' I queried back to the voice. I got no answer.

Now again, my glass scroll was still open. Now it showed me another moving picture that I remembered so well. That is because it had caused me much hurt and upset. There I was in the moving picture being told at the age of six by Aiden's father that in the real world we have to get jobs. Nobody could really go and play the drums and survive in the real world. Playing the drums was only okay for fun he said. Aiden's father said for us boys to get anywhere in life we have to focus on school (in particular spelling tests for Aiden) and doing our best. Whenever I remembered that discussion like right now, it caused me to feel upset.

My own parents told me not to worry about it and encouraged me to still play the drums but as I looked at the picture it broke my heart. Then it came to me like a bolt out of the blue. My parents had encouraged me. You could not see encouragement but you were able to feel it. What if it is the opposite of that? I thought to myself trying to be calm and not to get flustered.

Then I got it. I answered, 'Discouragement? Discouragement is the invisible poison to all man-kind?'

To that response the glass bubble lifted up to the roof top and another grey glittering bubble came out of the bubbling lake. Yet again curly writing appeared on the bubble ball in dark navy blue,

90

'Where is the greatest power in any Land to make great change?'

At that point I felt very deflated and stuck. I really did not know the answer to this one and I did not want to let anyone from my new list of friends down. That included: Gem-Star, the Smithereens, the Watchers right down to the Time-Keeper. The Glass scroll opened up once more and there I was with Aunt Jane in conversation. Now I remembered that discussion as it happened just before she tucked me into bed. Now what did Aunt Jane say to me that night? The pictures appeared to be moving and I felt so warm and cosy like I did in my bed. Just then the words fell off my tongue,

'Inside us,' I responded out loud. 'The greatest power is inside me and others to make great change.'

Up drifted the bubble ball to the cave's ceiling to form a beautiful crystal as the glass scroll rolled back up again. The voice had started to speak to me again. The Cave in a stern voice said,

'Jamie you have completed this challenge successfully.'

I noticed that a pale pink bubble ball drifted towards me. Why it was pink, I don't know? Then I stepped backwards and that is when things went wrong. I started to yell from the top of my voice, Help! Help me! But it was too late. Down, round and round and down and further down I went down the cold, wet slippery slide. Out of the Cave into some deep scary black hole!

Chapter 11 - The Rescue

Falling into a hole? Can you imagine that? I was fascinated as to why the last bubble ball was pink but after the shock of falling into a hole I couldn't think about that for much longer. I realised that something was not quite right. I was so disorientated and so would you be. I noticed that I was far under the boiling pool of bubbles. In fact I must have been underneath it. I started to get scared as I realised that all around me there were more icy walls with frozen creatures inside them.

'How did this happen to you?' I asked one of the creatures that looked so sad trapped behind the sheer iced wall between us.

Then I realised how I was so unbelievably cold. It was very cold down here compared to the top of the cave.

'Did you freeze? Is that what happened to you?' I questioned the frozen creature?

It suddenly came to me that I had to find a way out of there and fast or I would be in trouble like those poor creatures. I started to look around even though I could feel tears filling up my eyes. It was getting tricky to see with my blurry vision so I stood tall on my feet, blinked lots and started to walk around the frozen creature museum.

To keep warm I put my hands into my pyjama pockets. Suddenly it was when I did this my fingers found the little sack of gems that Gem-Star had given me. I quickly pulled the sack out of my pocket and opened it up to look at the gem stones. They were dazzling and the prettiest gems you have ever seen. The stones were cut in different shapes and sizes. Sparkling and dazzling. Then something marvellous happened. I must tell you. You won't believe what happened next. I started to feel warm and strong. That's right.

Strong, bold and courageous, I liked holding these gems in my hands as things were not so bad after all. There I was in a huge gigantic cave like a massive fridge freezer with iced walls and I felt not so bad after all. Of course I still wanted to get out as soon as possible. I held onto the gems as I walked around the cave to see if I could find an exit point.

Then I stopped in my tracks. There was the most beautiful creature you have ever seen behind the iced wall with droopy ears (like Aunt Jane's dwarf lops rabbit Cinnamon) and I could see how this white furry animal was crying?

As the tears dropped I saw the letters in frost on the ground; D, E, S, T, I, N, Y.

'Is that what you are called? Destiny?'

What is going on? Who put you in here and why?' I enquired.

Now as I asked the question I accidentally placed my hand holding the jewels against the iced wall and something bizarre happened. The wall started to crack! Huge cracks!

I then opened my hand and held the gem stones against the block of ice and it cracked even more! So much so I had to run away and stand back. From a distance I could see that the ice was starting to crash down and lots of dusty frost flew everywhere.

I hid behind one of the ice block poles with the gemstones keeping me warm. When I turned my head around the ice pole to peak over to see what was going on with the ice cracked wall I came face to face with a huge pair of black sparkling eyes and a black wet nose.

'YIKES!' I shrieked jumping out of my skin landing on the ice in my pyjamas.

Before me stood the fluffy white animal that been trapped inside the iced wall. As I jumped the creature jumped back too. It was cold enough but the white creature shook its head wildly from side to side splashing frosty ice and water everywhere.

'URGH,' I alarmed. 'That is freezing cold.'

The white creature noticing what it had done just bounced right over and decided to lick my face and attempted to get rid of the excess water on me.

'Oh Dear,' I wailed. I could not get over the size of this creature's ears. I knew in that moment that I wanted to save the other animals and that if the gems cracked on ice for this creature. It would work for the other trapped beasts too.

From one end of the cave to the other I kept running with the gem stones. I pressed them against the ice until the ice cracked and collapsed to set free different animals trapped behind the iced wall. Soon they were all set free and were shaking their bodies and ice splashes went everywhere. One by one each of these animals came to me. They understood that they were now set free as they wagged their tails or jumped up at me.

'Slurp! Slurp! Slurp!' the animals were drinking the icy wet water off the floor.

I soon realised that this was their way of celebrating and thanking me; splashing water and slurping from puddles.

'You creatures are really noisy when you are happy aren't you just!'

My furry new friends lifted their heads up and appeared delighted that I was speaking to them. I was curious whereabouts these creatures came from in the Land of Bong but before I could think about that the beautiful pink crystal bubble returned. It came floating towards me from out of nowhere.

'This is so magical!' I smiled at the pink crystal.

It came closer and closer and got bigger and bigger and before I could look at the animals to see what they were doing I couldn't see them anymore. All I could see was pink smoke everywhere. It was the pinkest fog and in my hand I just held onto the gem stones and closed my eyes tightly hoping it would disappear as fast as it had arrived.

'Hey everyone, I can't see you anymore? I hope you can still see me!'

When I opened my eyes I was astonished. There standing before me was the most adorable creature that was pink, fluffy with huge droopy ears and it had the most sparkling eyes I have even seen. The creature had a bubble ball on a chain over its neck. I looked at all the other animals noticing that they too also had a bubble ball on a chain around their necks now. The creature bowed down to me and then was joined by all the other creatures bowing down to me that had been set free. I pointed out,

'You don't have to thank me. It was Gem-Star's stones that helped us all.'

I suddenly noticed when I heard the sound of bubbles boiling that we were no longer in the bottom part of the cave anymore. We were back where my challenge had started in the cave.

The voice from the Cave of Bevel once again started to speak,

'Child you have broken the bondage and spell of old. You have completed your challenge and in addition to our expectations you have released Wisdom and her family. You have done well Child.'

The voice seemed less harsh and kinder towards me now than when I entered the cave.

'Her family thank you as they have been stuck in ice for years because they would not betray the Time-Keeper. They stood by their convictions (I have no idea what that means but I will look it up in a dictionary when I get home) by helping a dear friend of the Time-Keeper to escape. You have proven yourself worthy to progress onto the next task Jamie. You shall go onto The Land of Cogs.'

I noticed that on Wisdom's crystal neck collar her name was imprinted. I turned to Destiny. She too had her name on her collar.

'Your collars will help me to remember your names,' I beamed. It was like having my own gigantic pets!

'How do I get to the Land of Cogs? I asked. Is it far away from here?'

Without any time to question the cave voice anymore my white furry friend knelt beside me and with its massive floppy ears scooped me up and placed me onto its back.

'Oh my goodness,' I giggled. I got a huge lick on the face from the creature after being dropped onto its back.

'Destiny will take you onto your next challenge the voice from the cave responded. You must go there now!'

I held onto Destiny's woolly back and I wriggled forwards to use her collar as reigns.

'Whoopee,' I screeched as suddenly my new found friend started to jump and run with me through the cave.

'This is fantastic, whoopee! Yahoo!' I yelled out.

I did not take an inch of notice as to where Destiny was taking me. I must tell you. Never mind fun parks! This journey was the best fun ever!

Chapter 12 - My Surprise

My goodness!

'I'm FLYING!' I yelled at Destiny.

She continued to leap and carry me onto the next challenge. Truly, I thought I was flying in the air and the cold air on my face was so fresh I wanted to keep flying forever. Destiny loved to move faster than any animal I had seen before. My friends just wouldn't believe this I tell you! Suddenly the air appeared to be getting slightly warmer and I noticed that we were well out of the cave now and it seemed like we were inside the mainland. Before I had chance to think any more about where I was for the next challenge Destiny slowed down and walked.

'Where are we Destiny?'

Destiny did not speak but continued to walk me through a forest of Golden Trees. They appeared to be trees. Long tall golden trunks with golden branches that came out everywhere but they had no ordinary leaves on. They seemed to have golden circles all over the place and that is when I realised.

'They are not leaves Destiny! They are COGS!'

Yes that is correct reader. There on the branches of the golden trees were different shapes and sizes of Cogs. Scattered everywhere like leaves. That is when I heard voices and noises that seemed to create a tune.

'Cogs we are, cogs we turn, cogs we meet, cogs we whirl.' I asked.

'Which one of you is speaking to me,' I puzzled.

Then I noticed the second time as I listened to this tune that all of them were joining in the melody,

'Cogs we are, cogs we turn, cogs we meet, cogs we whirl.'

'Look Destiny!' I called her.

Destiny turned to look at the Cogs. As they spoke they moved in a circle on the branches of the golden tree. Destiny and I walked through the forest together and we listened to the tune again and again. Soon we came to a little hub of trees that Destiny led me to. It was magnificent and reminded me of the inside of my Grandfather's watch that my Dad gave me on my tenth birthday. The trees were so close that all of the Cogs were entwined and moving around each other. The different shades of gold were beautiful and it is one of the most glorifying things I have ever seen! It was a masterpiece.

You can imagine the surprise on my face when this masterpiece started to speak to me!

'Welcome our honoured friend. We welcome you to the Land of Cogs for your next challenge.'

'Thank you,' I said not knowing which part of the masterpiece to speak to as it was huge.

'Are you hungry Jamie?' I heard the Cogs masterpiece ask me.

In fact I think each Cog asked a different word in that question. I am not sure why they asked me this question. I replied,

'Yes I am hungry' followed by 'How do you do Cogs?' As I thought it to be polite and they were so kind in their welcome.

'We are delighted to meet you Jamie but, we must ensure you have energy and not waste time. Come closer to us and we shall provide you with a feast of goodness that will keep you strong.'

Destiny sat like a puppy dog and then stretched herself out like Aunt Jane's rabbits on the green lawn. I moved towards the Cogs masterpiece. Twirling and spinning around they went and they made the most majestic sounds I have ever heard. Then on the lower Cogs sparks started to fly out from everywhere.

'Whizz, pop, whizz, pop.'

The sounds alarmed me and I ducked down quickly.

'Whizz, pop. Whizz pop.'

Then there was a gigantic

'BURP!'

'Whizz, pop, whizz pop, 'followed by an even bigger 'BURP!'

I started to giggle and when I opened eyes there out of the sparks was a table covered with a gleaming gold cover made out of cogs! The table was covered with a feast of splendid foods.

'You must start to eat Jamie and help yourself to a Cogs-Feast' notified the Cogs.

Well I tell you this! I sat and munched through the most delicious foods I have ever eaten in my life! One of the treats melted in my mouth and it looked like a donut but in fact it was savoury. Creamy and buttery and tasted like my favourite cheese spread. Then another round treat appeared to have layer after layer of different golden colours in it and it looked like a gigantic cake. It was delightful! This truly was the best feast ever. As I tasted different slices each slice had different flavours from white chocolate to milk chocolate, to nutty chocolate to crunchy chocolate.

'Wow!' this is terrific!

The layered cake had wafer-thin paper layers and yet one bite took ages to munch. I couldn't resist taking bites out of different layers! The glasses made out of cogs had the most delicious fruity zingy juice in and yet it was not fizzy! It reminded me a little of Aunt Jane's traditional lemonade but this was so much nicer. Destiny was not at all interested in the feast and took rest. Perhaps she preferred different types of food being a magical animal. When I had finished eating I really did think I would burst.

***

The Time-Taker was livid as he turned to watch Jamie though a mist of smoke. There was Jamie as he finished his feast at the Land of Cogs. The Time-Taker was furious and as he swept around his purple hair was visible just outside his hood. He had a dreadful temper and was irritated beyond belief,

'I like to get other people's emotions into a bad state. Not my own!' he shouted.

'Enough is enough' he yelled watching Jamie speaking to the Cogs.

'You push me too far boy and if I cannot have the Time-Keeper and rule over the Land of Bong then no one else will. I have seen enough! I will not watch anymore of this ridiculous hospitality and generosity. All of the Lands will be mine. Each of you will bow before me with the Crown of Cogs. I will rule over you. If I do not have what I want then nothing will exist I tell you. NOTHING WILL EXIST!'

There was never enough for the Time-Taker and he did not like sharing anything. The fear of scarcity and bitterness drove him in how he wanted everything; especially to hurt the Time-Keeper.

Greed filled every cell of his body. He preferred to be alone if it meant he one day could control time and have things exactly as he wanted. It would be worth everything for him to have the Crown of Cogs on his own head.

'I will wear the Crown of Cogs Time-Keeper,' he boasted.

'Just you wait and see. I am strong and powerful and you are pure and weak Time-Keeper,' he spat.

'There is nothing worse in any world including an enchanted land than to forget who we are Jamie. And you are about to lose your mind!'

The Time-Taker in the misty smoke picture ahead of him placed his hands over Jamie's head. He moved his hands over and around Jamie's head and then a cloud of darkness fell into Jamie's head. 'You have lost everything now!' he grinned as he watched Jamie walk through the cog gates towards a golden path.

***

The Cogs-feast was soon over,

'Whizz, pops, Whizz pops, BURP!'

The food remaining all vanished with the table and chairs. The Cogs as they twirled elegantly around each other started to speak to me one by one. Each word became a sentence creating another speech,

'Jamie, you must enter through our gateway on your own for the next Challenge of Chime. Do not be fearful and you must resist all temptations that will be sent to test you.

'Oh my Goodness, Oh my Goodness,' I exclaimed.

The next thing was so magnificent. The Cogs that entwined each other and spoke to me started to part straight though their middle part. They started to play as they opened as a gate for me. As they opened they played the most beautiful music,

'I have heard that music before!' I expressed to the Cogs. It was a beautiful tune and sounded so lovely I didn't want to move from where I stood. It was the same music I heard from touching the Grandfather's Clock back in Aunt Jane's cottage.

The reality scared me of leaving Destiny and the Cogs. Before me was a golden pathway with scribbled black numbers that twirled and whirled over the golden flooring. I started to move myself forwards until I was standing on the flooring beyond the gateway. The gates started to close behind me and the music played on. The glorious tune. Gradually I saw the beautiful golden trees and Destiny disappear as the gates sealed back together. Before I had time to worry about being totally alone I heard a trumpet tooting louder and louder. It seemed to get nearer and nearer. I looked up and there heading towards me was the most enormous woven basket. It was falling from the dark sky above. I ran forwards and hid frightened of who it might be. I hid just off the path behind what appeared to be a huge golden shed.

'How strange this place is?' I whispered as I watched a man with a bright silver cape that shone in the moonlight climb out of the woven basket.

He stood for a moment on the golden pathway. I could not help but realise how he was so very odd. He had the most peculiar hat that had different shapes and patterns on it with bright colours. I think it even had colours that created flowers and they popped out at different angles. I moved forwards slightly.

'What is that? I wondered. His hat was made from huge balloons that made his head look so small. He looked like he had the tiniest head ever in such a gigantic balloon hat!

Chapter 13 - The Cuckoo Wizard

My heart was pounding like crazy. Who on earth was this man with a hat created from gigantic balloons? What on earth was he doing here? Suddenly I saw him walk towards me, down towards the Golden Shed's entrance. He took something out from his pocket. I took a deep breath in as I did not dare move. He unscrewed the door open with a key and then hundreds of feathers floated out onto the pathway and everywhere.

'What is all this about?' I muttered looking at the door entrance.

Multi-coloured feathers went everywhere! Then I heard the man speaking to someone,

'Tickety-Boo! How beautiful and how precious you all are my darlings! I love you so much and I will take care of you so well forever and ever.'

He carried on speaking,

'It has been such a long time hasn't it now but my Darlings haven't you grown so beautifully!'

Then the next thing I knew hundreds and hundreds of small feathery birds came flying out of the golden shed. They came darting out from all angles and flew everywhere at once. Hundreds of these beautiful birds zoomed and circled the golden shed and then the stranger in the balloon hat followed the birds.

'Why am I here?' I puzzled. These birds now sat all over the man and his hat. As if they were glued to his balloons (how on earth that hat full of balloons didn't pop is beyond me!). The birds covered the man, his bright silver cape and appeared to like him? They sat still now all around him. What a sight!

'Ouch,' I cried as out of the things in the sky now landed on my head.

'Ouch,' I feared not knowing what was going on.

I closed my eyes as things hopped around on my head jumping into my pyjama pockets causing havoc. I opened my eyes to find standing in front of me the man in the weirdest hat. His eyes were gleaming and seemed so huge it was unbelievable. Then this man bowed down to me moving his cape off his shoulders as he announced,

'O Guest. O Chosen One, How do you do? Are you Tickety-Boo?'

'O Guest, I beg you to forgive my pets. They love to play and enjoy company.'

I could not help but smile at this man standing in front of me. He continued on.

'It has been some time since my birdies had such a splendid head of hair to land on. You must be Jamie?'

'Who is Jamie?' I asked.

'Excuse me?' begged the Cuckoo Wizard.

'Where am I? I complained.

'Oh No!' said the Cuckoo Wizard.

'Why did you say that?' I asked the man with the odd thing on his head.

'You my young man have been enchanted by dark magic,'

'What's magic?' I was confused.

'This is the work of the Time-Taker!' he despaired. 'We must fix this fast! Quickly you must come with me so things can be Tickety-Boo.'

The stranger dragged me by my arm off the golden path into a green grassy area we both stood on. He held onto me tightly as these feathery things floated all over above us.

'This is a very sorry situation to be in. Indeed it is,' he uttered. 'Only a short time in the Land of Cogs and this is what happens to you. How dreadful indeed,' mumbled the man with a huge thing on top of his head.

The Wizard held onto Jamie by the arm, 'I do not want you to go missing anywhere,' he urged. 'Now then I think we are in the right part of the green for me to get some help.'

'Spell-binding, spell-breaking friends of mine,

I call to you now as it is just a matter of time,

Spell-binding, spell-breaking guides of time,

I invite you to attend as I call your rhyme!'

My arm hurt as the stranger held onto me. 'Why am I here?' I asked the man.

Huge holes appeared in the grassy green and out rolled massive balls with little people balancing on the top of them towards the stranger who held my arm. They travelled across the green quite fast as the glittering balls rolled beneath their feet.

'Thank pure magic for that! Tickety-Boo' he sighed. Soon the little people were in a semi-circle facing the Cuckoo Wizard as they balanced on their own ball.

'Why do they do that? I enquired. 'That is quite fancy isn't it moving around like that?' I commented. 'Do you know why I am here?' I asked the little people.

'Ssh Jamie,' said the stranger.

'What is Ssh?' I asked.

'Cuckoo Wizard and greatest friend it is only too good to see you. Just tell me how can we Spell-Guardians help you?' said the little man.

The Cuckoo Wizard adored the Spell-Guardians. They were so distinct in the way they always offered their help. They wore sparkling bright green outfits with helmets covered in grass. The grass was to ensure they were fully camouflaged as they worked in the Land of Cogs underground.

'Have you been over ground recently?' asked the Wizard.

'Not since we last saw you Cuckoo Wizard,' one of the older Spell-Guardians replied.

'I see,' said the Wizard. 'Well I beg of you my unique Spell-Guardians. I bring to you a most unusual case. This young boy Jamie has had his memory tangled by the Time-Keeper. As you are fully aware I am capable of counteracting the spell but I am very concerned about this.'

'What is your concern Wizard?' the female Spell-Guardian enquired.

'Indeed this is a bad case. He cannot even recall his own name the boy is beyond vulnerable. I don't even think he could manage to eat, drink or have a conversation let alone complete the Challenge of Chime!' the Wizard despaired.

'And how may we serve you Wizard?' the smallest Spell-Guardian asked.

'Spell-breaking guidance is what I need to confirm with you and then again Spell-binding seals. If I am correct we cannot get this wrong or Jamie could remain without his memory for the rest of his life? That is not a Tickety-Boo situation my friends for Jamie?'

'Wizard that is correct,' the female Spell-Guardian confirmed.

'Cuckoo Wizard, you must ensure that the Time-Taker is not cursed in anyway during your spell-breaking action. As you may recollect the spell-breaker if it includes a curse (even a silent one) from yourself the curse can revert into you and it will become you. Both you and the boy shall result in total loss of memory,' the oldest Spell-Guardian declared.

'It is good for you to counsel me as you are aware I have been incredibly focused with my magic in another universe with my enchanted cuckoo birds. What about the spell-binding seals? The Wizard questioned.

'Ensure Wizard that you let go of any bitter thoughts towards the Time-Taker. The Time-Taker would be only too glad if you held onto your anger, annoyance and frustration regards to what he has done to the boy. Those thoughts will not allow the stronger magic to work and supersede the Time-Taker's enchantment,' warned the oldest Spell-Guardian.

'When you cast your spell Wizard be certain to flow like the balls beneath our feet when we are working continuously moving forwards. That is all we guide you in our dearest friend,' the little Spell-Guardian announced.

'Tickety-Boo! Very well my unique friends,' I listen to your wise words and I shall now set to work on Jamie.

The Spell-Guardians gently pushed their balls forwards with their green ballet slippers that moved their glittering wheels to move. They circled around the Cuckoo Wizard and Jamie as the Wizard started to chant his magical words.

'By the Land of *Gnoble*

G-enante

N-umoura

O-bera

B-canda

L-Tamala

E-La CUBO

Memories of old and memories of few

We command you return

Renew, RENEW!'

The Spell-Guardians nodded at the Cuckoo Wizard as they moved their feet quickly out of their circle to return to the underground. They balanced on their shining balls of light and waved just before they vanished into the huge holes in the grassy green. Once they entered the holes they sealed up on the grassland. There was no a trace they had ever been present.

I opened my eyes to find a strange man with three bright red bow ties on his shirt standing before me. On his head was a most fabulous massive balloon hat.

I spoke, 'How do you do? My name is Jamie' as I waved to him feeling a little confused about where I was and who this stranger was.

'Tickety-Boo Jamie! My name is the Cuckoo Wizard. I am a Cuckoo-Clock Wizard, but if you prefer you may call me Cuckoo or Wizard. Thank goodness you are alright?'

I couldn't help myself, 'That is a rather different name,' I exclaimed.

'Rather unusual I know but I have that name with honour,' he boasted.

'It does not matter that you don't remember what you have just experienced,' he smiled. 'It is perhaps better and more Tickety-Boo that way!'

'What do you mean? And what do you do?' I enquired.

'What do I do? Well, I am the trainer of all the Cuckoos that must be trained for all Cuckoo clocks throughout the world,' he continued.

'It is a glorious thing to do, to spend so much time singing and helping my cuckoos to sing sweet tunes. It is not an easy task to do you see. Each day is a challenge. I train my cuckoos to act very still inside the clock and then at the correct time to sing to their audience. When they enter their own home and clock they are trained to go out to other Lands and Universes.'

'Many of them live in a land called Switzerland. It is very Tickety-Boo in Switzerland, he boasted'

At that point I could not help but to hold and look at these wonderful tweeting birds. They dived between each other and sang sweet chirps to each other.

'Switzerland is a place I have learned about in school,' I remembered.

I recalled to the Wizard, 'Switzerland is a country not a world. Usually inside cuckoo clocks the birds go Cuckoo, Cuckoo.'

'Ah, yes indeed they do! After they are trained in many other skills first, I teach and train them that skill to sing Cuckoo, Cuckoo.'

I enquired, 'What skills do you teach the birds first Wizard?'

He smiled as I took interest.

'Tickety-Boo! Well to start with my lovely Cuckoos are trained in happiness. Then the ability to stay still inside the clock when they live in another Land,' he answered.

I pointed out, 'That must not be very nice staying still all of the time.'

'Of course it is not nice' said the Wizard sharply. 'But you do know that my birds are magical. Obviously they do not stay inside the clock all of the time?'

Now that was most fascinating news to me, 'Really?'

'Truly?'

Curiosity filled my heart.

'Jamie, the skills of the Cuckoos are not just to tweet 'Cuckoo' as they are trained in the first instance. They are also trained in flying around their owner's home to magically bring gifts to their owners. Gifts that they bring (his whole head and body is covered with Cuckoo birds right now and I can just see his face) include; joy, inspiration and creativity. They fill the home with these things and that is because they love their owners more than you can imagine. One day one of my cuckoos helped a little girl with her Easter-egg competition and she won it! Another Cuckoo bird helped one little boy with his piano practice and he became a wonderful piano player! How Tickety-Boo is that?'

'How fascinating is this news!' I expressed.

The Cuckoo Wizard then told me,

'I have been waiting for the key to be twisted for some time so I could come back to the Land of Bong to take my little friends with me. They have waited a long time for me to return. Now I must take them back to my Cuckoo School for their training. I would love to speak to you some more but I simply must take my little friends back home.

While the key is twisted it is possible for me to come and go. The time will come when I will be stuck and unable to return when the Challenge of Chime is completed.'

I felt sad to know that my new friend had to leave me. I so wanted to know more about the Cuckoo Wizard and just before I could find out anymore he had to leave me.

'I am sorry that you must leave so soon,' I mumbled.

'You must not be sad Jamie. It is not good-bye. It is a see you later' assured the Cuckoo Wizard. Besides that he told me,

'You can choose what feelings you desire to hold onto Jamie. If that is the case then choose the best feelings. Like me I choose Tickety-Boo! Besides that you have the Challenge of Chime to complete! You must go on!'

Within a few minutes the Cuckoo Wizard had hopped back into his woven basket and it was surrounded by birds. I had never seen such a delightful sight and it was just so awesome. The noise of

'Tweet-tweet, tweet-coo, tweet-coo, tweet-tweet,' was blissful to my ears.

Then, all the birds started to flap their wings together as the Cuckoo Wizard stood with his gigantic balloon hat in the basket. Off into the air their sailed. Up, up and up they climbed until I could no longer see the feathery multi-coloured basket or the Cuckoo Wizard.

***

The Time-Taker picked up the beads from around this neck and pulled towards him the clock-face that was at the end of the beads.

'I thought having no memory would be the greatest punishment for you Jamie. To not remember your precious family, why you are here and even your own name.'

'Obviously it was not enough! That foolish Cuckoo Wizard will be punished after I've finished with you boy!'

'It is time for you to take the opportunity of a life-time Jamie. To take a very different path like mine and for your own decisions to corrupt you,' he cried out.

'I have seen your type before and your wavering about everything shall bring you DOOM!'

'BAM!'

All that was left was black mist.

***

Chapter 14 - Heebie-Jeebies

I strolled along the golden path on my own and as I walked I counted the different numbers. From where I was standing now I could no longer see the golden shed or the entrance to the Land of Cogs. I felt so alone and empty. All around me it appeared dark and black apart from the golden pathway I walked on.

'Two, four, eight, ten' I counted as I carried on walking.

I think I must have walked for quite a few hours and felt so lonely and worried about where I was and what was I going to be doing next. This was not the type of place to be wandering about in your night clothes. It was scary and cold.

Out of nowhere I could see a faint light ahead of me. It was the only bright thing I could see apart from the golden path that I walked on. As I approached the light I could make out something underneath it. It looked like person but as I got closer I realised it was in fact a harp. A rather huge golden harp and besides it was a golden stool to sit on.

I was just about to sit down on the stool (I had been walking for hours and deserved a rest) when I heard a voice say out loud,

'EXCUSE ME!'

I jumped out of my skin and started to shake.

'I am sorry,' I answered, 'where are you?'

'Never-you mind where I am,' the voice cried out.

'How simply DARE you!'

Now I was feeling very nervous and had started to shake.

'I'm sorry,' I repeated.

I started to walk away back onto the golden path. Just as I started to walk away the voice kept shouting,

'Don't you dare walk away from your challenge!'

'How DARE you! How simply DARE YOU!' the voice shrilled.'

My butterflies started to go in circles making me feel faint and that is because I knew I had to complete this challenge. This was scary being shouted at with no clue where the voice was coming from. 'Who are you?' I asked.

The voice did not give me much time to think about my heebie-jeebies for much longer. The harp started to play magically by itself and then the voice said,

'How dare you, be you,

How dare you indeed?

How dare you be here?

Sitting beside me!

I know I can tempt you

To tempt you indeed

How dare you, be you

You have heebie-jeebies!'

Then the voice started to laugh outrageously loud and it sounded louder than my dad's monster lawnmower.

'HA, HA, HA, HA HAAAAAA.'

The harp stopped playing and then in front of me out of nowhere appeared a fridge.

'Magic,' I guessed.

I couldn't help but be curious about the fridge as I was so thirsty after my long walk on the golden path. I started to walk towards the fridge feeling very confused and upset. When I opened the fridge it had inside the most amazing fruit juices in different shaped cups with fantastic smells coming out of the cups.

'I'm thirsty.'

I went into the fridge and as I was getting closer to reach a cup out to drink. I stopped still. I don't know what made me to do this but I just stopped going for the cup of fruit juice.

I put my hands back down beside my side and just stood there staring into the fridge and then I closed my eyes and did nothing. It didn't take very long and the harp started to play and the voice cried out in a rather harsh voice again,

'How dare you, be you,

How dare you indeed?

How dare you be here?

Sitting beside me!

I know I can tempt you

To tempt you indeed

How dare you, be you

With your heebie-jeebies!'

Again the harsh voice cackled out, 'HA, HA, HA HAAAAA!'

Then, the most dreadful thing happened the fridge disappeared and instead before me stood a jar full of ugly insects. Right in front of me! It was enormous. These ugly insects had beetles and creepy legs with hairs poking out of them and hard shells that covered their bodies. I had never seen such an enormous jar of insects before and or any of that kind. These bugs were crawling all over the insides of the jar and that is when I noticed other things inside the jar.

There was a red rose with insects crawling over it and beneath rolled up in a tight little ball was a Fur-Fog. It wasn't moving it was just in a tight ball with his little ears. I noticed him because quite a few insects were crawling on his tail.

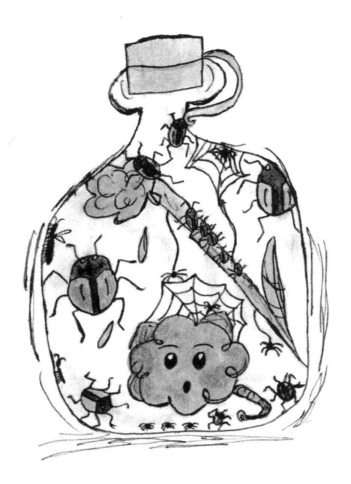

I had never been so scared in my life before and I was more nervous than you can imagine but I could not bear to see the Fur-Fog stuck inside this jar.

'You are unkind!' I shouted out to the voice that cackled from the magic harp. 'How could you torture this creature?'

Although I was full of nerves I knew I could not leave the creature inside the jar for a moment longer. The jar was enormous but I walked around it and tried to figure out a way to climb to the top to open the lid and allow the Fur-Fog to escape.

That is when I had an idea. I pulled out the gems that Gem-Star gave me. They felt so warm in my hands and these gems were cut in such a way that I could use them a bit like nails to climb up to the top of the jar. My decision was made. I held a jewel in each of my hand and then started to use them in the glass to climb the Jar of Insects. I could not use anything to support my legs (on a tree I would often use a branch or two) and was hanging here, there and everywhere as I climbed.

'Whoa,' I slipped a few times as I tried to hammer the jewel into the glass jar.

At one point I was so afraid of falling down as my legs felt so heavy. Pyjamas were not ideal clothes to climb this huge jar in. I moved the jewel up to a higher level so I could keep climbing. My mistake was looking down and seeing in the distance the harp. It was so far away now.

'This is terrifying compared to climbing trees!' I stressed.

At one point I was so close to the top of the jar but my body was just hanging from the jewels that were in the glass because I just couldn't carry my own weight anymore. I was dreading and I knew that I could fall at any moment. I was petrified. As I hung from the jewels in the glass the insects crawled around on the inside of the jar. I am sure they were looking at me, hoping they could climb on me too but the glass between us kept them away from me.

Hanging onto this gem was making me want to let go. My arms were aching all over and I just wanted to let go. I could feel my hands slipping.

'No, No NOOOO!' I cried out and suddenly out of nowhere, I pulled the jewel out of the glass and stuck it into the top of the jar lid. It was a miracle.

'Yes,' I shouted. I pulled the gemstone out after I managed to pull my body up onto the top of the jar.

'YES!' I celebrated. I had done it. I was on the top of the jar.

On top of the huge jar I breathed deeply just to get my breath back as I glanced around.

'How on earth will I manage to get this massive lid off this jar? It must be possible,' I insisted.

'Someone must have fixed it on it the first instance.'

I was determined that the impossible was possible. The ugly insects stared at me as they climbed over the bottom of the lid.

'Urgh!' I grunted.

I could not stop thinking about the poor Fur-Fog in his tight-ball position at the bottom of the jar. I started to knock and bang on the top of the lid to get his attention.

'Bang, Bang, Bang!'

The Fur-Fog didn't move anywhere. Then I spotted a huge hook that linked through a metal bar on the rim of the jam jar.

'How on earth do I get that un-hooked?' I grumbled.

Things just seemed to be getting worse. The Harp was being horrible to me as I walked on the lid.'

'You are useless. You are no good. Just you wait and see. You will fall off the Jar,' it started to laugh again.

I tried climbing up to the jar lid and now finding an awkward hook. A hook too huge for me to un-hook! I got an idea but it was just far too dangerous and the most foolish idea I've ever had. My idea was that if I sat on the edge of the jar and lowered my body down I could get hold of the metal hook and then to leap off the side of the jam jar.

'My weight might pull the hook out?' I predicted.

'I think I would be heavy enough to manage that,' I estimated.

Those insects were creepy and I needed to act to save the Fur-Fog. So off I went with this crazy idea (if my mother could see me now she would be furious with me) and I dangled my legs over the edge of the jar, just until I could reach the metal hook held in place. I was scared because if this worked all the insects would be free to climb out of the jar and to crawl on me!

'Yikes,' I muttered 'How awful would that be?'

I looked at the brown furry ball. A scared curled up Fur-Fog. In that moment without thinking any further I grabbed the metal hook and I jumped off the side of the jam jar.

'Argh' I roared out as I jerked down suddenly on the metal hook as it came free out of its slot. The hook being free threw me down hard against the glass. My body bounced off the side of the jam jar and it hurt!

'Help, Help!' I cried.

I swung around I was waiting to see what was about to happen with all the bugs. Especially now the jar lid was off. The strangest thing occurred. One by one as the insects climbed out of the jar; they disappeared into a ball of grey, dusty smoke.

'POOF, POOF, POOF, POOF!'

One by one the bugs vanished into grey dust they climbed out of the jar. The bugs never got their freedom.

Eek! I felt something tightly whip around my waist.

'HEEEEEEEELP MEEEEEE!' I screamed as I could see myself falling off the jam jar upside down.

'Help MEEEEEEE,' I repeated. Then I stopped as I realised I was not falling but being carried upside down? It all happened so quickly until things started to make sense. I was now looking upside down at the brown Fur-Fog. He started to jump up and down and swing me side to side.

'PLEASE Put me down!' I cried out

'Put me down Fur-Fog.'

And so he did, he just dropped me onto the floor in a heap.

'OUCH!' I wailed to him clearly expressing that you can't do that to children. I looked into his dark black eyes and said,

'That was so scary it is the scariest thing I have ever had to do before.'

Before I could get too excited about the Fur-Fog's freedom the Harp started to play the same music but before it started to sing a massive grey cloud of smoke filled the area we were standing in. The Fur-Fog ran away down the golden pathway out of sheer fear leaving me on my own. Out of the grey smoke walked the Time-Taker with his hood so low down I could not see his face. As he lifted his hood he brushed away some of his purple hair that appeared just in sight from his cloak. He walked towards me and then sneered,

'And so Jamie, did you like my musical Harp? Doesn't it play the most wonderful music and sing the most wonderful song?'

I started to quiver as his hood was just empty and filled with darkness. I felt guilty, cold and full of fear as he approached me.

'No, I did not like your musical harp or the song it sings,' I responded valiantly. I hoped he could not see my true feelings.

'Is that so?' he urged. 'Well let me tell you something Jamie. You may have brought freedom for the Fur-Fog but it is not over between us yet. Do you think for a moment I will let you succeed in the Challenge of Chime? Do you have any idea of what that would mean?

'Yes I do know what it means and that is why I will keep going with the Challenge of Chime' I answered.

'Ha-Ha! So you know what this would mean for me to lose? And yet you stand there before me and tell me you think you have a chance of winning? You think you will get through the rest of the Challenges!' he started to laugh again. 'Ha, ha, ha, ha, Jamie you do make me laugh!' he sneered.

'I will try my best in the Challenge,' I announced.

The Time-Taker came very close and whispered something in a very low sharp voice.

'Would you like me to tell you a secret that the Time-Keeper kept from you Jamie? She is so powerful with that Crown of Cogs and yet she kept this secret from you. Do you know who in the ancient times won the Challenge of Chime? And who won the Time-Keeper at each and every task? Do YOU?' he taunted.

'No. I don't know anything about this secret or who won the Challenge of Chime,' I told him the truth.

He then got close to my ear and whispered, 'It. Was. ME, he revealed!'

He turned away and started to stroke the beads that hung low from his neck. I noticed some red rose petals drift to the ground as he said,

'The Time-Keeper has filled you with false hope and has false pretences Jamie. Besides that, if she wears the Crown of Cogs and has so much power, glory and ability then why did she not BANISH ME! FOREVER?' he stormed.

I did not think it wise to interrupt the Time-Taker especially when I knew it was him who had kept the Fur-Fog prisoner inside that jar of insects. I just looked at him pitifully.

The Time-Taker then stepped up to me and as I tried to dodge him he seized me by my neck,

'If you think the Time-Keeper is so kind and lovely and gracious Jamie. Then tell me this, please do. WHY DOES SHE NOT COME AND SAVE YOU RIGHT NOW?'

I could feel my tummy full of zooming snakes. I found it tricky to keep breathing. I had no idea how to respond to all these terrible things the Time-Taker was saying,

'Stop it!' I sobbed with tears welling in my eyes.

He continued on, 'If the Time-Keeper was so brave then why did she not complete the Challenge successfully herself?'

Then he added, 'Jamie if you treat me as your Master I shall save you from the disgrace of losing the Challenge of Chime. I will create for you a better, richer and more powerful life than any you have ever known or heard about. Come with me and you will live or die in your quest!'

The Time-taker then said,

'You will have all the most wonderful gifts and hearts desires that the Time-Keeper would never offer you. EVER! That includes trees to climb, toys you want, you will be that Superhero. The best gift is POWER!'

I have never been fearful as I was right now. I could not go with the Time-Taker as it was clear he compromised everything and everyone he ever knew. I felt sad that the Time-Keeper had not told me she had lost the Challenge of Chime in ancient times. I responded,

'No! I will not follow you or go anywhere with you freely. I will not work with you ever. I want to complete the Challenge of Chime and I want to go home,' I announced.

The Time-Taker dropped his hold on my neck and started to pace around me in a circle. He stepped forward, closer and closer he came and then he whispered in a very controlled tone,

'Where will all this moral high-ground get you now Jamie? Think carefully! This is the END for you now you foolish little boy. Do you think that people in this world are fooled by your morals? You ARE IMPERFECT!'

I could feel my eyes were blinking lots to stop me from crying. He continued to behave in his evil ways,

'Do you think you can keep secrets from me? DO YOU? DO YOU? I know all that is Jamie. A fine example of this is how you really would love it if you were an only CHILD! Nobody else to get on your nerves! Wouldn't you just love that?'

My heart was pumping faster and faster now as I panicked how the Time-Taker could read my own thoughts about my sister Emily. He screamed,

'You will go somewhere where there is no hope for you ever to return home. I will send you to the Still Lands. Everything is stuck and unable to grow or mature. You will be there in stillness and darkness. Other universes will bow down to me and only ever me. I shall wear the Crown of Cogs.'

My neck was still sore as he waved his arms up and then higher up into the air. I could see lots of smoke starting to spin around in a whirlwind of dust.

I whimpered and closed my eyes trying to be brave and trust that all would be alright. Before I could open my eyes to see what happened next I was swept up in a whirlwind. The whirlwind was fierce and fast throwing me from side to side and I didn't want to open my eyes. I shouted,

'STOP! Somebody Help me! Somebody Help ME! PLEASE!'

Backwards then forwards. Faster and faster.

My whole body was being thrown around and turned upside down.

The whirlwind was harsh and threw me around and around.

'THUMP!'

I was thrown to the ground.

'That HURT!' I moaned. 'Where on earth am I now?' I whimpered as I opened my eyes.

The first thing I could see right up tall and in front of me outlined in the darkness was a gigantic waterfall. I got to my feet to get a closer look. Huge rockery surrounded it. The odd thing is how it appeared to have different shades of water frozen from the top of the waterfall all the way down into the rock pools. I gasped. The water was not moving. It appeared totally still. I turned my head and looked around me and said,

'Oh, No!' Everything around me was not moving. The trees outlined in the darkness were still. There was no wind and the air never moved.

'I feel like I'm stuck on a still postcard,' I whispered.

It was dark with no signs of life and everything around me was totally still.

Chapter 15 - The Time-Keeper's Promise

'This is very sad,' I stared into the darkness where everything around me was lifeless. I pottered about the waterfall. It appeared so beautiful with different shades flowing from the top of the waterfall to the bottom.

'What happened here?' I whispered hoping that someone would answer me.

One good thing is that the Time-Taker was nowhere to be seen but I knew in myself it would be for a short time until he returned. I felt sad as out of the dusty earth flowers with heart shaped petals appeared still. No smell. Sadness filled me as the flowers did not look real. They reminded me of my Mother's dried flowers with no smell or fragrance; pretending to be real. For the first time since beginning the Challenge of Chime I really felt deserted.

'Will anyone find me or help me?' I wondered.

I moved around the Still Lands and all I could think about the people I loved and cared about. The fun times I had had in the past with my friends. Climbing trees and going camping with friends. I would miss them all if I didn't get out of the Enchanted Land of Bong by winning the quest.

Again tears welled up in my eyes as I thought I would never see my family again. I thought about Emily my little sister. She did get on my nerves so often at home. Now I was so sorry for having ill thoughts about her. I wanted to get back to Emily. I missed her and truly I would never want anyone to hurt my little sister.

Just then in that moment I quietly whispered out loud to the still air hoping that someone would listen to me.

'Please be with me and help me to not be abandoned. I'm so scared in this Still Land' I expressed.

'Help me and show me how to complete this challenge. How do I get free?'

As I said the last sentence, I moved around the dusty earth and rocks in the darkness looking for signs of life. Nothing moved and no sound. I decided to return to the frozen waterfall. As I approached the waterfall I could see a whirlwind of smoke arising over by the rocks. I kept on walking faster and faster knowing something was wrong

As I walked closer right in front of the waterfall I sensed I was no longer on my own. The waterfall appeared to be getting brighter. I was amazed by the multi-coloured patterns on the waterfall. Different colours all blended together like a jigsaw puzzle; it was so beautiful. As I touched the waterfall I started to hear in a gentle tone the Time-Keeper's voice speaking to me from somewhere?

'Jamie, I am unable to be with you in person throughout this challenge but my presence will never leave you; I am with you always. I promise to be with you not only at those times of your journey when I know you need my help but during those times when you are successful.'

My heart warmed as she continued, 'I will not be physically present but I promise you that at all times during your journey; I will be with you to encourage the wisdom as a child you already have.'

I watched the whirlwind of dust get faster and faster and I knew something was not right. As I walked to the waterfall I felt stronger for hearing the words from the Time-Keeper again. My heart although troubled was filled with love knowing that the Time-Keeper was with me. I stepped towards the waterfall in the darkness less troubled filled with trust. Then something spectacular happened. Out of the still sky and the clouds that never moved a light shined through the Land. A truly bright and magnificent light that was full of stars with its brightness glowing onto the waterfall. It was such a large beam of warmth and it shone on my face, making my freckles glow. It beamed strong heat onto the Land of Stillness and the waterfall was multi-coloured.

Suddenly I felt something move behind me. I was leaning besides the rockery and I noticed how waves flowed from the top of the waterfall to the bottom. All of the colours seemed to be moving around and around each other it was just so amazing. My wonder was soon broken,

'So there you are BOY! I am so glad you have waited for me to deal with you once and for all!' The Time-Taker looked vicious as he stepped out of the whirlwind.

126

I turned towards the wave of different colours in the waterfall because I knew something was about to happen, I could sense it. Then, one by one pieces of the waterfall started to move outward towards the Time-Taker. Hundreds of fluttering butterflies everywhere. They were huge gigantic butterflies. One by one they went and flew outwards. Soon there were multitudes flying fast from the waterfall. I turned towards the waterfall in awe realising they had once formed the multi-coloured frozen water. They had created the waterfall! How? I have no idea. Faster and faster they flew off towards the Time-Taker. There were so many distracting him he could not visibly see me anymore and he was cursing and fighting with them,

'You will have more than broken wings now,' he warned 'I'll crush you all!'

I had no time to dwell on the sight. During all this time the glorious light continued to beam on the Still Land and the waterfall.

'How did that happen? I questioned'

I suddenly realised an opening in the waterfall.

'It's time for me to move,' I declared.

I dived through the centre of the waterfall quickly so that the Time-Taker would not be able to see me anymore. I kept running. Meanwhile some butterflies returned to the waterfall opening to close it fully; whilst others continued to dart towards the Time-Taker.

I could hear from behind the closed waterfall,

'No! No! No! TAKE THAT AND TAKE THAT YOU NUISANCES! I'LL STAMP ON YOU ALL!

Chapter 16 - Jangle, Furl and Scamper

'Phew,' I muttered.

I felt relieved as I didn't want to watch the Time-Taker's attack by butterflies anymore. Rather than waste time I walked into the depths of the waterfall wondering what would be coming next.

'How do I get to my next challenge now? I gasped. I was very aware of how more time had gone by.

He takes my time away from what is most important, I thought.

'I must focus on the challenge,' I vowed.

My thoughts were interrupted,

'CLUNCK, CLUNCK, CLUNK!'

'CLUNK, CLUNK, CLUNK, CLUNK.'

'What is that noise? Who is it?' I said hoping somebody would answer.

'CLUNK, CLUNK, CLUNK, CLUNK!'

Nobody answered so I thought it best to keep quiet.

'CLUNK, CLUNK, CLUNK, CLUNK, CLUNK!'

How odd? I thought. I looked in the distance and for sure I could see things dropping from a height down from the great peaks of the waterfall rockery. I kept walking towards the noise and then I saw what was falling out of the rockery.

'Fur-Fogs,' I revealed.

I picked up my walking pace to get a closer look at what the Fur-Fogs were up to. Why they decided to fall from great heights only you could imagine. As I approached these chocolate brown furry creatures with black sparkling eyes I could see they rushed to what appeared to be clusters of Fur-Fogs.

Soon, I was standing the middle of lots and lots of Fur-Fog flocks and they appeared to be in some type of meeting?

'Hello. My name is Jamie and I wondered if at all possible you would kindly help me. I'm lost you see and I need to return to the Challenge of Chime as quickly as possible?'

As I spoke out to the Fur-Fogs I could hear one or two of the younger Fur-Fogs talking to their parents.

'Mother, he has very long legs compared to me? Why has he not got any fur or furry ears?

Another asked, 'Do you think he has a short tail?'

The older Fur-Fogs just smiled at their young family and explained,

'He is our Guest and he is not a Fur-Fog, he is a boy.'

Suddenly from above me I heard a further

'CLUNK, CLUNK, CLUNK.'

In front of me were three mature Fur-Fogs. They had masses of fur all over them almost like a round-fur ball with small feet with long tails.

The Fur-Fog flocks quietened down as the three Fur-Fogs approached.

Each of them in turn knelt down before me.

'Guest Jamie,' one of them said.

'Welcome O Chosen one' greeted another.

The third Fur-Fog took his time to rise and as he did he said,

'O great and wonderful child. Welcome to our home and thank you for your great works so far.'

Now this came as a surprise to me,

'Great works?' I asked.

The third Fur-Fog called out, 'Scamper.'

Out of one of the clusters came the Fur-Fog that I recognised as the one who had been trapped in the jam jar of insects. The older Fur-Fog said,

'I am Scamper's father and you may call me Jangle and this is my wife Furl.'

At that Furl came forwards and kneeled down.

Jangle added, 'You saved our son who has been captured for many years and trapped by the Time-Taker. The Time-Taker has much regret, envy and greed in his heart but is also full of anger. Some years ago when Scamper tried to help another in the Land of Bong he was captured by the Time-Taker. The Time-Taker was furious that our child had helped. He cared for someone like you who had come to our Land with the 'Twist of a Key.' As punishment knowing how Fur-Fogs dislike insects (I understand you call them creepy crawlies?) Scamper was held captive inside the jam jar for many years until you set him free.'

I was taken aback by how the Fur-Fogs used the term creepy crawlies?

'How do you know we call insects' creepy crawlies? I asked.

Jangle said, 'Our friend from another universe informed us when she was set free that Scamper was captured before she returned to her home land. She explained how he had a magic rose placed inside the jar to give him air and food to live in the jar. It was torture.'

I got curious. 'Someone else has been here before me? I enquired.'

Jangle walked closer to me and we walked together into the waterfall. He explained,

'The only way you can come to the Land of Bong Jamie is with the Twist of a Key. Yes. Another has been here before you but a promise was made by her never to share that we live in this enchanted land. Not to another living soul.'

This was fascinating news to me and my heart was beating so fast thinking about who else had been here. I wondered how long ago it had happened.

Furl then added,

'Jamie, we must ensure that you are prepared and fed well ready for your next challenge. Time is so precious and although we have much joy to see you for all that you have done for us. We must keep to time and get you to the next challenge. First we shall feed you and ensure you rest for a short time. To make sure you have your strength renewed.'

Scamper and the rest of the Fur-Fogs took me to a dark wooden place that looked like a castle. It reminded me of Fort William a play fort that has different activities to play on back home. Inside the wooden castle there were slides, runways, ropes and different activities to do. What I found incredible is that the Fur-Fogs could walk slowly but when they wanted to get anywhere fast they curled up into a ball and rolled! There were quite a few of the Fur-Fogs rolling around the wooden castle and rolling down the slide. It was so terrific to watch! Scamper then spoke to me,

'We all use this to exercise and we must keep ourselves full of energy Jamie. We have a duty to roll and ensure that the Cogs in the Forrest that you have already visited are spotless and clean. We use our tails to climb the trees and we roll all over the Cogs to ensure that nothing stops them from working. We visit the Cogs when it gets dark at night to ensure that they are immaculate so that they can function to keep time perfect.'

I found this most fascinating I must say.

'Why at night?' I asked Scamper.

'The Cogs need to speak as one in their land and must grow continuously to ensure that time goes perfectly. At night they do not realise that we are cleaning them spotless as we are dark and fast. Like you Jamie, the Cogs have restful times at night to recover and it is the best time for us to do our duties.'

Scamper then added as we sat down at the wooden table to eat and drink,

'The Time-Taker wants the Crown of Cogs because whoever has that same crown has power to create things in time that can be for good or bad.'

I looked into Scamper's mop of brown fur intrigued by what he was telling me.

I enquired, 'Is it true that the Time-Taker won against the Time-Keeper in the Challenge of Chime?'

He continued on,

'Once upon a time, the Time-Keeper and the Time-Taker were not always enemies,' he mentioned. 'The Time-Taker won the Challenge of Chime Jamie but how is another story. The Time-Keeper is of great importance and cherishes honesty and integrity. Her enchantment is that she creates trust and love forevermore.'

'How did the Time-taker become so evil to lock you in that jar of insects? I asked.

Before Scamper could answer my question we got interrupted as there was a Fur-Fog announcement by Jangle.

'Fur-Fogs of the Butterfly Waterfall, I welcome you at this table and our Guest Jamie. We wish him well after his meal with the next quest in the Land of Clock Face and home of our dear friends the Snuggle-Buttons. Here is to Jamie and our victory!' Jangle beamed with delight.

At this point so many Fur-Fogs got excited that they rolled around all over the place with their tails coiled around their bodies. They were quite excitable creatures.

I now asked Jangle a different question, 'How did Scamper the Fur-Fog get captured by the Time-Taker?'

Jangle responded, 'Jamie, as Fur-Fogs we roll around as part of our duty; often at very high speed. When Fur-Fogs are young they require much discipline to roll properly. Rolling around for many of our young Fur-Fogs causes them to be quite dozy and docile. They are vulnerable and in a dizzy state.'

Now I had heard this term before and I could not believe that Jangle was saying young Fur-Fogs were docile.

I clarified, 'Docile?'

Jangle continued,

'Jamie they roll all night and if they are docile and dizzy they are incapable of making good decisions. Our young are influenced easily unlike mature Fur-Fogs.'

Following our meal and Scamper complimenting me on my pyjamas I was taken by the family of Fur-Fogs to a multi-coloured bridge at the end of the waterfall rockery.

'This is where you need to start the next Challenge of Chime,' Jangle assured.

The Fur-Fog creatures all started to roll and wave goodbye to me when Furl passed me something into my hand.

'This will help you when you think you least need it Jamie,' she advised.

I looked into my hand and there was a long chain with an arrow at the end of it.

'Thank you Furl,' I commented not having any idea as to how I would use such a gift.

As I stepped off the bridge onto wooden flooring I turned to wave again to the Fur-Fogs. Sadly I was unable to see the Fur-Fogs after crossing over the bridge. The bridge started to break up as butterflies flew up into the air and towards me. I had just walked over a bridge of butterflies. How special is that? I would never get to do that at home with my friends.

Chapter 17 - OUCH!

Dark clouds surrounded the Time-Taker as he viewed Jamie stumbling along the path towards the Land of Clock Face. Fury, bitterness and burning anger were just a few of the feelings the Time-Taker experienced right now. There was less and less time for the Time-Taker to act and cause disruption and this bothered him greatly. More petals fell down to the ground from his red rose. Suddenly the Time-Taker's expression changed. He started to smile with his hood down low over his face. It was evil when he laughed creepily and started to point his fingers,

'My idea is pure genius and a dreadful way to hurt you. You asked for this you foolish BOY!'

He schemed to remove Jamie from his next challenge and from life itself. The Time-Taker took out his hands from beneath his gown and started to shape a picture in the grey smoke. The smoke formed the outline of an ugly beast with massive muscles, huge legs, big hefty arms and a bulky body. Then the Time-Taker blew the picture in the direction towards Jamie into the Land of Clock Face.

***

I soon came across the most gigantic wooden and golden door that you have ever seen in your life. As I faced the door I wondered how to get through it. It was huge and enormous panels of wood ran down to the ground from a great height. I just spotted a rusty door handle and imagined how I could open it from where I was standing when the ground started to shake.

'Thump, Thump, THUMP!'

My fear kept me still. I hoped Destiny had returned?

'Thump, Thump, THUMP!'

I turned around to find an enormous Giant standing tall above me.

'Oh No!' I whimpered.

Immediately I started to look around for somewhere to hide. The Giant started to stare downwards at something? Perhaps it was me? I gasped and then ran into the corner of the wooden door way so that I would be out of his view.

'Bang, Bang, Bang!'

He hammered the door with a massive club and started shouting,

'WARGH, WARGH, WARGH.'

I could feel my whole body shivering with fear and nerves so much I wasn't breathing.

'What am I going to do now?' I moaned.

'Help me, help me please,' I whispered shuffling into the corner of the doorway as much as possible so that the Giant could not directly see me.

The Giant had horrible teeth that were black and he drooled everywhere from his mouth when he shouted.

'WARGH, WARGH, WARGH!'

I knew that the Giant wanted to capture me or even possibly SQUASH ME? The boys at school would never believe this in a million years I thought to myself.

'Now what do I do?'

But it was too late. I had to make a rush out of the doorway for my life as the Giant laid down so he could easily poke me with his finger in the doorway and grasp me better.

'OUCH!' I shouted as his finger pushed me into the wall.

'HELP! THAT HURT!'

I never knew how huge a Giant's hands were. He had massive, big, thick, fat rounded fingers and thumbs. What an ugly beast I thought as I ran as fast as I could around the corner of the big wooden building. The Giant decided now to stand up again to catch me.

Around the corner I kept taking deep breathes in and out.

'What am I going to do? What am I going to do?' I repeated.

Thinking and wishing someone would tell me. I had never faced such a huge Giant in my life before and uncertainty crippled my body. I was not ready for any of this he was so much bigger than me. School did not teach me or any other ten year old how to handle a Giant! Something in my pocket stabbed me as I moved. It was the Fur-Fogs gift. I pulled it out of my pocket and looked at it. I started to think how I could use this chain and arrow to get me out of this mess? The wooden floor was shaking with the Giant's massive steps shouting,

'WARGH, WARGH, WARGH!'

He stomped around the entrance looking for me. I got the arrow and chain ready still not knowing what I would do with it. The Giant's feet stomped around the corner now in front of me and I just knew some action taken would be better than no action. The worst thing would be not to try my best (that is what my Aunt Jane tells me about everything I do; even when I clean my teeth!)

He was enormous and so angry and boisterous as he came towards me. I couldn't even shout out for help because I was terrified of him and his size. He had huge metal breastplates clamped over his chest and metal plates over his knees. He leaned forwards to try and pick me up. I took a deep breath in and whipped the chain around above my head and threw it with the arrow towards him. Now what happened next was truly amazing. The arrow went straight between the Giant's eyes and he fell over backwards with a look of shock, his eyes frozen still. The ground shook and I seriously thought it was an earthquake. Many wooden panels broke and smashed as he fell down.

Before I moved I quietly tried to see if the Giant's chest was still rising up and down. It was safe. As I approached the Giant something really spooky happened. The Giant started to break up into a cloud of smoke particles. The cloud of smoke particles was right above my head. Black and grey dusty smoke hung over my head.

'Whoosh' it vanished.

All that was left behind was the chain and arrow on the empty floor space where the Giant had been. I grabbed the chain and arrow and ran around to the door entrance of this large wooden door. I banged my fists on the door like crazy.

'Let me in, let me in,' I cried out.

I kept banging on the door with all my might.

'There are Giants out here! Please somebody let me in, let me in!' I repeated as I pushed with all my efforts.

Then without any warning the floor opened beneath me.

'WOOOOOOAAAAAHHHHH!'

I screamed again, 'WOOOOOAAAAAHH!'

Down into darkness I fell as the wooden floors beneath my feet collapsed letting me go further and further down into a hole.

'Help me! Help me!' I shouted out.

My feet were up in the air and I could feel myself falling down, down and further down into a dark hole. The air was making my hair stand upwards and I must have done at least five somersaults forwards.

'Boing, Boing, Boing, Boing, Boing, Boing.'

I realised my body had landed on a trampoline of some sort and I was bouncing up and down into the air and back down again.

'Boing, Boing, Boing, Boing, Boing, Boing.'

As I bounced up and down and up and down I heard someone calling out,

'Places everyone, quickly please get to your places! Our guest has arrived and we must ensure the next challenge is completed so no time is delayed.'

'Boing, Boing, Boing.'

I was slowing down now on this trampoline of some description.

'Boing!'

I heard lots of children making squeaky noises,

'Move out of my place,' a male squealed.

The female squeaky voice said, 'I must stand here this is MY place.'

'Phew, I said. Hurray that I'm not moving anymore!'

No more bouncing.

'Welcome Jamie, said the man with the long wriggling pink nose. I am Mr Snuggle-Button and this is my family of Snuggle-Buttons. You are late! We have been expecting you for some time.'

Chapter 18 - My Squealing Friends

I bounced my way off my landing place that was a bright green triangular trampoline. I couldn't help but notice that the room was filled with the most beautiful bottles in a range of shapes.

'Welcome to the Snuggle-Button's home in the Land of Clock Face,' a little Snuggle-Button squealed.

I smiled a huge smile for they were funny creatures. The room was decorated in the most peculiar bottles. I must say how I was absorbed in the bottles around me. They were curly, long, fat, thin and so many different colours. I then realised that the Snuggle-Buttons each wore a little glass bottle around their necks on a little chain. They did dress quite odd possibly because they were such a peculiar shape. In fact a Snuggle-Button's shape reminded me of the letter S when they stood on one side towards me.

'Mrs Snuggle-Button come quickly we must prepare Jamie for the challenge as soon as possible. Where are you?'

Mr Snuggle-Button had a squeaky voice too but it was not as high pitched as the female Snuggle-Buttons. I heard Mrs Snuggle-Button call out,

'I'm here my Dear. I was just arranging the bottles in order.'

I think I would find it tricky to live with Snuggle-Buttons as my ears would pop too much with all the squealing. Mrs Snuggle-Button stood before me now in the brightest purple outfit,

'Hello our marvellous Guest,' she announced as her pink nose wriggled all over in delight.

'Hello Mrs Snuggle-Button,' I said.

I could not help but love and be fascinated by these cute creatures. I approached as I watched them,

'May I ask you a question Mr and Mrs Snuggle-Button?'

Mr Snuggle-Button replied,

'Of course you may ask us Our Chosen Guest Jamie.

'Why do you have so many bottles in the Land of Clock Face? I mean what do you do with them all exactly?' I was so curious.

In a squeaky voice rather more delighted I had asked Mr Snuggle-Button answered,

'Each bottle has something precious inside it Jamie and they hold very special messages for each person. They wear the bottle for eternity!'

Now this was fascinating stuff I thought.

'Eternity Mr Snuggle-Button? What type of message do you need to keep for eternity?' I enquired.

Mr Snuggle-Button's nose was wriggling all over and I tried desperately hard to listen now, as I so wanted to understand.

'Many of us need to keep certain messages in our hearts every day, in every week of our whole life-time if not longer,' he said.

His eyes twinkled with excitement as he could see my curiosity. Mrs Snuggle-Button then gracefully breathed in and sat down beside me adding,

'He is not being as clear as perhaps he should. The messages are like promises that one must never break or rather like rules. They keep you protected wherever you go in your life-time Jamie. Many may think the messages are not for them and that is their choice to disregard them. An example of this is our enemy the Time-Taker. He has chosen his desire for 'power' over love and harmony. We in the Magical Land of Bong live by these promises. It is as the Time-Keeper would say a part of our ancient way.'

This discussion made much more sense now that Mrs Snuggle-Button had explained things to me.

'How on earth do you manage to put the messages or promises into the bottle of peculiar shapes?' I asked.

I stared at all the bizarre shapes and different colours of glass.

'I'll show you,' suggested Mr Snuggle-Button.

He took me to the most delightful thing I've ever seen in my whole life.

'Wow!' I said 'This is wonderful.'

Behind the Clock face there was a large wheel and inside it was another smaller wheel. I was fascinated by the colours that were created between these two wheels as they spun around each other. One wheel was going swifter and faster on the inside whilst the outer wheel was going steady at a slower pace. Golden stars and streaming colours quite like a rainbow were created on the back of the Clock Face. You could see the outline of the numbers from the inside of the clock that was in fact on the outside of the clock face. I remembered that on the outside of the clock face these numbers were black but on the inside they were golden and sparkling like fire. These wheels turned around and around.

Mr Snuggle-Button explained, 'This controls time as the inner wheel spins around and the outer wheel goes steady. As they both move together in motion time is created, days pass by as they both go forwards.'

Mr Snuggle-Button took a bottle from Mrs Snuggle-Button's hand and removed the lid with his nose. Then he carefully moved his nose towards the beams of multi-coloured light between the two wheels. His nose darted into the rays of colour that whizzed around in between these two circles that moved forwards with energetic speed. Stars and sparks flew everywhere and plenty of glitzy dust flew onto us all who stood watching.

Mrs Snuggle-Button sweetly boasted,

'Only Snuggle-Buttons are gifted at collecting messages for our bottles of promises Jamie. Our noses were created especially to sniff upwards in time to capture the promises. Our talent is to capture and pass these messages or promises to all future generations in our sealed bottles. Our noses adapt easily for the most unusual shaped bottles. We never a problem with that,' she smiled.

Now the Snuggle-Buttons had me hooked!

'Wow! That is very clever to be able to use your nose like that. How long do you keep a message in your nostrils?' I asked.

Mr Snuggle-Button stood tall (which was rather tricky with him being such a usual shape like a teapot) and looked peaceful about something. Then he lifted up the bottle and sneezed into it. Stars fell out everywhere as he did so. Quickly he placed the lid on the top of the bottle.

'We hold the message in our nostrils long enough to enjoy and understand it but it is for us to pass it on to others,' Mr Snuggle-Button emphasised the 'pass it on to others.'

He added, 'This is what we do all day long and we love it!'

The younger Snuggle-Buttons were looking at me now with their twinkling eyes and they dazzled like my gems. Their noses' were wriggling all over with excitement.

'Who do you give these bottled messages to?' I asked.

'Mrs Snuggle-Button in her excited squeaky voice said, 'We send them to all the other Lands Jamie. Gem-Star intends that one day we will send them out to other universes too. It will bring love between our planets and universes,' she approved.

Mr Snuggle-Button advised me,

'Jamie, you are very close now to completing the Challenge of Chime. The Time-Taker is not happy about what we Snuggle-Buttons do or intend to do in the Land of Clock-Face or beyond in our Enchanted Land of Bong. In fact, he detests my family and our roles.'

I was so eager to know why the Time-Taker disliked the Snuggle-Buttons or their remarkable bottles so I enquired,

'Why is that?'

Mr Snuggle-Button explained,

'Many years ago the Time-keeper and the Time-Taker were both followers of our ancient way. The Snuggle-Buttons have pure hearts. He dislikes us for our pure hearts as we are known as the 'Core' and heart of the Land of Bong. Snuggle-Buttons bring hope and peace. The Time-Taker detests our work as he has selfish desires and he never puts others first. His motives are all wrong.

Before I could get my next question out Mrs Snuggle-Button said,

'Jamie, you must go forwards now and complete your quest. We will not see you after the next challenge as it will lead you into the Land of Moon Dial if you are successful. We are we are sure you will be successful.'

I really liked Mrs Snuggle-Button and her purple outfit and I didn't want to leave my new friends. I wanted more time in the Land of Clock Face. Mrs Snuggle-Button appeared to sense my sadness about leaving them as she fussed over me and admitted,

'We have a gift for you Jamie.'

She then put a dark ribbon with a bottle hanging on it around my neck. After the ribbon was tied she put the bottle underneath my T-shirt so that the bottle was not visible. My bottle was awesome as it was a spiral twist and had rainbow colours floating inside the glass.

'Gosh! Thank you Mrs Snuggle-Button for such a lovely present, it is so fantastic with all those different colours,' I delighted.

The Snuggle-Buttons took me up front and close to the two spinning wheels and then they explained,

'Jamie we must leave you here on your own for this challenge now. We are unable to help you in anyway whatsoever. The task will start when you put your hand out into the centre of the spinning wheel that goes incredibly fast. If I remember correctly there is nothing else for you to do after that. Everything happens for you.'

I hugged Mrs Snuggle-Button good-bye and waved at all the little ones as Mr and Mrs Snuggle-Button moved everyone back behind a wall covered with glass bottles. I could no longer see any of them.

There was no time to waste so I walked forwards towards the spinning wheel taking a deep breath in before I placed my hand into the centre of the fastest wheel.

'Zap, Zap, Zap, Zing, Zing, and Zing.'

I felt like I was now flying high up in the air and the feeling was unbelievable!

'Zap, Zap, Zap, Zing, Zing, and Zing.'

I WAS FLYING! There was just me and I was pulled into the middle of the spinning wheels? I turned my head and there was nothing behind me anymore. The brightness of the multi-coloured lights sparkling was unbelievable. Stars were everywhere and for sure I was inside the wheels. It was unreal to be flying.

'Whoopie!' I cried.

I was flying! All I could do was let my legs dangle in the air using my arms like a pair of wings without feathers. Suddenly a deep voice, out of nowhere started to speak,

'Explain why you are here BOY!'

Now I started to get nervous as I was floating in the midst of the wheel vibrating with the deep voice vibrations.

'I am here for the Challenge of Chime,' I declared valiantly.

'Then you must indeed answer the following riddle to enter the next Land BOY!' The voice announced.

'First you must tell me this. Where do other's put their focus upon in the wheels of time and why?'

Second you must tell me this.

'What must others focus upon in the wheels of time and why? Why do they not do this?'

Now I am ten years old (I know you already know this about me) but this type of question is not the type of question I would ever be asked in Scouts, school tests or by teachers. This question was tricky and not quite like those adventures in my comic books. Spiderman never answered that type of question on his mission to save Mary-Jane from the Green Goblin.

From in between both wheels I watched the inner wheel going fast, really fast and the outer wheel going slowly. What does this mean I thought? I tried to remember what the Snuggle-Buttons had told me about the wheels of time and how they provide promises and messages.

'Something to do with a life-time and eternity,' I whispered.

I watched as the inner wheel went so fast and the other wheel went quite steady. I was puzzled as to my own position in the two wheels and as to what the questions could mean? I carefully took the gems out of my pocket as I was floating up in the air with my legs beneath me and felt their warmth in my hands for comfort.

The voice announced, 'Take care with your responses. BOY!'

I held onto the gem stones feeling scared of what was going to happen next. Suddenly the most spectacular thing happened. As I looked at one of the gem stones I could see right through it. I could see that the small circle whirling fast had people inside it? I could see how people were rushing driving cars. Parents dashing from work to collect their children from nursery. Lots of people were rushing down Oxford Street in London shopping. I lifted the gem stones up further to view the outer wheel. In the outer steady wheel there was a beautiful castle, garden with lots of grassland and flowers. There were fairies and birds dancing between the fountains in this beautiful garden.

'What does this mean?' I commented.

I spotted something. There were paths made out of stars and flowers going from the inner circle all the way into the outer circle. They formed a gateway. The people in the inner wheel could easily walk on the luxury gateway and reach this lovely place but they were so busy with life they didn't realise it even existed.

'This is so unbelievable. Why can't the people see it?' I queried.

I felt fortunate to see the gateway that was so obvious especially when no one else appeared to see it.

I will look out for that path next time I play out with my friends,' I declared.

The voice informed me again,

'First you must tell me this. Where and why do others put their focus upon in the wheels of time? Then you must tell me this. What must others focus upon in the wheels of time and why do they not do this?'

I then answered clearly and with confidence,

'Firstly people put their focus on living in the small wheel of time and that is because they are so busy to look anywhere else. These people simply cannot see the path. They are far too busy to even notice that this path exists.'

I continued to answer the questions,

'People in the small wheel must focus on the passage way. That beautiful gate-way allows them another lovely destination. They don't see it. That is because they are just too busy each day to notice it exists. They are too busy spinning in the small wheel of time to notice that there is indeed another awesome wheel spinning around them.'

Suddenly, I felt myself being sucked through some type of tight straw tight tunnel. I kept turning around and around with such bright lights beaming I had to close my eyes.

'WHAT?' I screamed.

I can compare this experience to one similar like a massive spider being hovered up in a vacuum cleaner. I could not open my eyes as it was such a bright light; it was blinding. I could hear female voices in the midst of me being pulled through this tube.

'Do you think he is arriving here soon?' asked a female voice.

Another female voice announced, 'I think he will arrive shortly.'

'WHAM!'

After being crushed to pieces in the tunnel now a tighter pressure took over all over the whole of my body. From top to toe I felt squashed and I took what I thought was my last breath.

Chapter 19 - The Cup of Harm

The Time-Taker filled with fury. He had his hood low down over his pale complexion. He stormed around in his cloud of smoke as he prepared to meet with the Time-Keeper. Petals drifted into the cloud of smoke from his rose as he brushed back his purple hair underneath his hood. The opening of the butterfly waterfall had annoyed him beyond belief and he knew now what he had to do. He had no doubts as to how those butterflies had been brought to life after years of being frozen still. He threw his beaded chain and time-less watch over his cloak as the smoke cleared. He was ready and he swiftly moved into the Time-Keeper's presence as she sat in glory on her golden throne.

The Time-Keeper sat gracefully and patiently expecting the Time-Taker's arrival. She noticed how he avoided eye-contact with her as his hood was filled with darkness. His voice was full of scorn as he began,

'YOU have broken the ancient way Time-Keeper and you know there is a cost when you do not keep the rules of ancient time. You will not DARE to ask me why I am here after what you have just DONE!

The Time-Keeper smiled softly and listened. She would not raise her voice to his. She did not desire to anger him further and in a quiet voice when he stood still she replied,

'You and I both know that I did not help Jamie through the Butterfly Waterfall. Jamie felt my presence with him in the Land of Stillness but you know I did not use any enchantment to help him escape.'

'ENOUGH! The Time-Taker spat. Regardless of what you say Time-Keeper there have been RULES BROKEN! You know the consequences of interfering with the Challenge of Chime. You and I both know that if one is to help the boy during the tasks that there is a price to be paid. I have come here to see that the price is paid Time-Keeper!'

The Time-Keeper whispered knowing he was trying too hard to not make eye-contact with her,

'You know how I did not create the ray of light that opened up the Butterfly Waterfall to set Jamie free? So Time-Taker why do you come here?'

His dark hood dropped back slightly to reveal the Time-Taker's purple hair.

'If one helps another during the challenge Time-Keeper they must pay the penalty. You must pay that penalty Time-Keeper. The rules were written in our ancient way. Are you not going to follow through what was ordained Time-Keeper? As you drink from the Cup of Harm that foolish boy continues with the challenge. To think the impossible is possible is foolish. As he tries to be successful you must drink from the Cup of Harm.'

The Time-Keeper lowered her eyes for a short moment before she responded,

'Time-Taker if this is to be done I will surrender to ensure that the Challenge of Chime continues for Jamie but know this first. I have hope and belief in Jamie. You make fun of the impossible being possible but I believe Jamie will complete the Challenge of Chime victoriously. Jamie's heart is shown in his actions not words and he follows the difficult road to become victorious; not the easy one.'

She stood and walked elegantly towards the Time-Taker. He stood in front of her not wanting to look in her soft eyes. He knew that her pure motive and presence was powerful. Her smell of flowers and freshness made him bitter and angry when he thought of the years he had been banished on another planet. As they stood in the centre of the wooden hall the Time-Keeper raised her arms and out of the wooden flooring a golden fountain appeared. It was covered with golden numbers and jewels all over it. The water was icy blue and overflowing everywhere. It was spectacular. Springs of water formed a beautiful sound in between the noises of trickling water. At the side of the fountain was a golden cup on its own and the Time-Taker picked it up. He raised his arms and smoke covered the golden fountain changing the icy blue water to a dark polluted substance. He dipped the cup into the fountain and then put it into the Time-Keeper's hand.

As soon as she grasped the cup he stormed away from her,

'You broke the ancient rule Time-Keeper and you must drink now from the Cup of Harm. You are foolish for helping that stupid boy. If you do not drink now that disgraceful child cannot complete the Challenge of Chime!'

The Time-Keeper took the cup delicately and then carefully walked with it towards her chair as he stood watching her. She climbed the jewelled stairs and sat down in her beautiful gown. The Time-Keeper turned towards him,

'Victory will be Jamie's Time-Taker.'

She raised the Cup of Harm,

'Your wickedness will be shattered and you will disappear back to your own planet, in your own smoke.'

Then she drank the dark substance from the Cup of Harm. The Time-Taker stood in front of the waterfall as the Time-Keeper suddenly dropped the Cup of Harm and sluggishly fell into her chair.

The Time-Taker slowly raised his arms and the golden fountain disappeared back into the wooden flooring out of the room.

'Thank you for that Time-Keeper,' he commented.

The Time-Taker glared at the Crown of Cogs with pure desire to possess it. He wanted to take what he wanted right now in this moment but he knew he could not take it yet. He climbed the jewelled steps and stared for a few moments at the angelic Time-Keeper.

'It is sad that it had to come to this,' he whispered. 'I will always love you even though you rejected me?' he kissed her on the cheek. She was frozen cold.

The Time-Taker stood up and with a wave of his arms created a passage of darkness. He ran into the smoke knowing there was no time to lose.

***

Chapter 20 - A Fiery Furnace

I opened my eyes to find myself laid on my back and there was a huge golden telescope above me.

'How did I get here?' I questioned.

I blinked and then jumped as a cute pixie looking creature was staring right into my eyes just inches away from my face! I didn't move. I blinked again and then there was another peering at me. Again I blinked and another face appeared very close. Three in total were now glaring at me. Eventually one of them spoke,

'Welcome to the Land of Moon Dial Jamie. I am Gem-Sun and these are my sisters: Gem-Cloud, Gem-Moon and I know you have met Gem-Star already. We are so pleased to meet you! Did you enjoy your travel in the telescope?'

I stumbled up on my feet smiling in disbelief that my body had squeezed through that golden telescope.

I confirmed, 'You are Gem-Star's sisters?

'Indeed they are,' claimed a voice I recognised.

I quickly turned to see Gem-Star standing behind me. She was a beautiful pale pink with hair to match. She walked quickly towards me and gave me a tight hug before admitting,

'Jamie, a planet is missing and that can only mean one thing. I believe on this visit the Time-Taker's powers have somehow increased. He was banished to another planet and the planet vanishes when he returns to the Land of Bong. Now the problem is that at this stage of the challenge we should be able to see his planet in the universe from our telescope.'

Gem-Sun in her sweet tone announced, 'We watch other planets and wider universes through our Telescope. We have been keeping a watch on the Time-Takers planet at the request of the Time-Keeper.'

Gem-Moon explained,

'One day we intend to send our bottled messages over to these planets with eternal promises. We are working together to make this happen.'

Interestingly Gem-Cloud added,

'The Time-Taker was banished to planet seven and we warned the Time-Keeper when it suddenly went missing.'

'What has the Time-Taker done to gain such power and for us not to see his planet returning to the universe?' I questioned.

I was keen to know if and how the Time-Taker could get stronger.

Gem-star appeared sad when I asked her this question she explained,

'Jamie, he has by some means taken strength from the Time-Keeper. There is no other way he would have accessed such power. His planet should be in full view now. He may have caused her pain or even death.'

'I don't believe it,' I babbled as my eyes filling up with tears.

'Death?' I choked.

The Gems all nodded their heads at the same time and I could see tears in their eyes too. Gem-Star walked towards me,

'Jamie, you must complete the final challenge otherwise you will not get home and worse things will come to be. The Time-Taker will gain even more power and be able to destroy other universes and time as we know it.'

I stood tall like my mother asked me to when something important was happening at home. I swallowed my salty tears and said courageously,

'Quickly! Show me to the next challenge.'

Gem-Star walked ahead of me as the lovely Gems walked me through into an enormous wooden room that had a moon and sun moving around each other. They were a centre-piece attraction in the room.

'This is why our home is called the Land of Moon-Dial,' exclaimed Gem-Star.

'What does it do?' I enquired.

'It aligns time perfectly in the Land of Bong,' she continued.

'The Moon and Sun Dial ensures that timing is perfect throughout the Land of Bong and in all worlds,' she assured.

My heart was racing when I thought about my family and what could happen if I did not get through my next challenge.

'To enter the next challenge you must walk into the Dial,' said Gem-Star.

She added, 'You still have a chance of successfully completing the Challenge Jamie, if you move quickly.'

As soon as they said quickly I waved as I left them. I ran straight into the Dial without having any chance to say proper goodbyes.

Inside the Dial everything around me disappeared. No voices, no noise. It was like I was in space with total silence around me? I walked below the Moon and Sun Dials as they kept to time going around each other and then I saw the most mind-blowing thing. There was a magnificent fire burning underneath the two Dials. I moved as close to the fire as I could because I could see something burning inside the fire.

Then I gulped realising what it was, 'A key?'

There inside the fire was a key about the size of my whole arm. I recognised that key.

'That is the Grandfather Clock key!' I gasped.

In front of my face created from the flames came words of fire that were so clear. I read different sentences.

The first was, 'You must hold the key and open your heart.

The next sentence read, 'To hold the key you must be free.'

Followed by, 'You are chosen.'

In my school in London we have had local Firemen come and speak to use about how dangerous fire is.

'I must follow these messages to win this challenge.' I thought of all the people who had brought me here to this moment on this challenge.

Without hesitancy I jumped into the fiery furnace full of flames knowing that was the only way I would hold the key. There was nowhere for me to go but forwards into the fire. I was surrounded by brightness and glowed in the flames,

'Wow, I'm standing in the fire. This is unbelievable! I'm not burning?' I observed my skin again.

The flames did not burn me and my pyjamas were still intact too! I was totally safe so I moved fast to grab the key. As I walked around inside the fiery furnace I felt stronger than just moments before I jumped into the flames. I could see the Sun and Moon Dial above me moving around each other. My fear was less now I'd got the key (it was quite heavy) ready for the next adventure so I jumped back out of the flames.

'Now what would my friends think about this,' I beamed looking at the enchanted key that brought me into the Grandfather's clock.

'They would probably think what a fool you are because you did not complete the Challenge of Chime,' the Time-Taker suddenly jumped out before me.

His hood was filled with darkness as I stood in the brightness of the flames with the magical key.

He was horrifying, 'Do you honestly think that you will defeat me? You are a mere boy! One stupid, idiotic and simple child. I have already defeated the Time-Keeper and she is no longer around to help you Jamie. Now it is time for me to claim and wear the Crown of Cogs. I will RULE OVER ALL TIME AND UNIVERSES!'

He was full of selfishness and as my friends would say at school quite a big-head. Thrusting his head forwards to scare me I caught a glimpse of purple hair from beneath his hood. The Time-Taker had purple hair? This was not the time to be curious I thought. My heart was racing fast.

The Time-Taker's went quiet and then he darted towards me like lightening. As he came forwards at me I put my hand out to push him away snapping his beaded necklace. Beads scattered everywhere and a faceless clock rolled onto the floor. I threw myself right back into the flames dragging the hefty key with me.

'NOOOOOO!' the Time-Taker cursed as he dived towards his faceless clock. In that moment, I realised something was wrong. Perhaps it was that he could not touch me or the key whilst I was in the flames? I could see him outside the flames shouting,

'My Time-Sourcer what have you DONE? Do you think you are untouchable Jamie? I will find you and take my revenge. I will have the Crown of Cogs!'

The flames burned high off the ground whilst I stood inside the fire. The Dials rotated above me. I turned to see how else I could get out of the fire without the Time-Taker catching me. My heart was pumping and there was nowhere for me to go. What had the Time-Taker meant about defeating the Time-Keeper?

Then it happened. Noises came from above me as the Dials started to swoop lower around each other. The Sun and the Moon came lower down. They were in perfect balance. Down, down and further down the Dials came towards me.

The Time-Taker was furious, 'THIS IS NOT THE END BOY. DO YOU HEAR ME? THIS IS NOT THE END. I WILL HAVE MY REVENGE!'

It seemed to me from inside the fiery furnace that something had happened to the Time-Taker as all I could see was darkness.

I stood still holding onto the key tightly as the Moon and Sun Dial came lower and lower until they swooped around me. Then there was silence. I could no longer see anything or hear anything.

Everything went quiet. Everything was still. All I could remember was the feeling of the Key in my arms as I tightly clutched it as close to my body as possible as the flames continued to burn.

Chapter 21 - The Magic Medicine

I found myself clutching the golden key against my body and the flames were gone. I was now right back at the start of my adventure in the grand hall at the Palace. I'd done it! I had successfully completed the challenges.

'Whoopee!' I shouted in excitement.

I could now return home.

'The golden key must have magical powers to return me to the Time-Keeper's Palace,' I stated.

I couldn't wait to share all about my journey with the Time-Keeper when I suddenly remembered what Gem-Star had told me. I turned my head and was in shock. There was the Time-Keeper slumped with her head hanging over to one side in the chair. Her eyes closed.

'Wake up Time-Keeper! Please!' I cried as I ran towards her with the golden key. By accident I kicked over a cup that was on the floor.

'Time-Keeper? Time-Keeper?' I shouted.

'Can you hear me? I did it I helped others through the challenge. I've got the key! I'm back Time-Keeper!'

The Time-Taker was still and her face was the palest white with bluish lips. I felt numb as I could see from her body that something was terribly wrong.

I looked at her feeling hopeless not knowing what to do. I cried out, 'Help! Help! Somebody HELP US!'

Nobody heard me shouting. I cried and held the key to my chest.

'Why did this happen to you?' I sputtered.

I could not understand why she had left me. Salty tears rolled down my freckled cheeks. My body was heaped over hers with my tears pouring down onto the Time-Keeper's gown and onto the golden key. The key felt warm.

And warmer. Suddenly it was too hot to touch so I moved back.

'What's happening?' I puzzled.

I stood back and watched the golden key sparkling brilliantly as it lay over the Time-Keeper's body. Rainbow coloured rays of light came into the room over the Time-Keeper as she lay still.

The stained glass windows blew open as gusts of wind entered. A stern voice echoed into the room,

'Pour from the Key elixir into the Cup to awaken her.'

There was no mistaking it. A voice was instructing me to somehow use the Key and the Cup to wake the Time-Keeper.

'Pour?' I thought.

I dashed down to pick up the golden cup. I picked up the key realising that there was bubbling fluid inside the key? I realised that there was a seal on the bottom of the key. I lifted it as I placed it over the golden cup as it rested on the jewelled steps. Drops of golden elixir dribbled into the cup. It was like an old watering can!

Quickly I dropped the key and took the cup to the Time-Keeper. I lifted the cup and golden elixir to her bluish coloured lips to pour it in her mouth. Then I waited. And still I waited. I stepped down with the empty cup in my hand feeling so desperate hoping it would work.

Slowly as nothing was happening I turned my back to the Time-Keeper.

As I walked a shadow followed me on the wooden floor and it wasn't mine. I turned around slowly to see the Time-Keeper's eye-lashes fluttering. She had opened her almond brown shaped eyes.

'Time-Keeper' I yelled out in delight.

'Time-Keeper you are alive!' I screamed out as I ran to cuddle her.

'Thank you Jamie,' she whispered. 'Thank you for being so determined.'

I will not forget how 1 felt in that moment when the Time-Taker opened her eyes to speak to me. It would stay with me forever.

'My life was saved by your care and attention Jamie,' she breathed.

'I surrendered to the Time-Taker with him thinking he was the most supreme in his knowledge. He is not wise with his knowledge and that is because he forgets there is a much greater power. The power of love is the strongest force beyond dark enchantment and always will be. The Time-Taker clings to the darkest power and it consumes him. He is unable to let go of it Jamie.'

As I hugged the Time-Keeper she explained how she had been faced with the Cup of Harm as the Time-Taker believed she had broken the ancient way according to the Land of Bong.

'But Time-Keeper,' I enquired, 'Why did you drink from the Cup of Harm when you say it was not you who helped me to escape?'

She replied softly,

'Jamie. I know how enchanted magic opened up the Butterfly Waterfall. I know that this magic and power was beyond my own. Much stronger and deeper than the Time-Taker's tactics,' she answered.

'As a result of that greater magic being used I had to follow through with any consequences of that decision, even if it was to cost me my life.'

She smiled at me. 'It was also a test of my own love and honour for a much greater purpose. A plan created by one much greater than I. This was not just about you completing the Challenge of Chime Jamie.'

'Who is greater than you Time-Keeper?' I questioned.

She stood tall, 'That is another story for another time Jamie. Now we must prepare for you to return home.'

We walked together across the great hall carrying the golden key together to a multi-coloured glass window. In the window wooden frame there was a key lock that was rather huge.

'This is the lock we need to use for you to return home Jamie,' she informed me.

We placed the key into the lock and the Time-Keeper hugged me as she pointed out,

'Look Jamie! There are others who want to wish you well on your journey home too. I peeked behind the Time-Keeper and there were all of my friends from the Land of Bong. They had returned from all their own lands to say farewell.

'How amazing! How did you all get here so fast? I asked.'

The Time-Keeper in her dazzling Crown of Cogs delighted,

'Jamie, you should know by now how the Land of Bong is one full of enchantment and magic.'

All of my friends were waving at me and I opened my arms as I ran towards them. Gem-Star stood with her emerald green hair besides her sister Gems who danced all around me. Gem-Cloud exclaimed,

'The Time-Taker's planet has returned back to the universe Jamie. We can see it through my golden telescope. After you left us all we found on the floor was this.'

Gem-Cloud held up a red rose stem that had no petals remaining on the flower itself.

The Time-Keeper said, 'A red rose was returned to the Time-Taker a long time ago. It only has life in the Land of Bong when the Time-Taker returns by the Twist of a Key.'

Before I could ask any questions I was distracted by the Fur-Fogs who were spinning around on floor doing some type of celebration dance. Behind this dance, in mid-air I could see the Cuckoo Wizard in his basket waving at me with a gigantic smile on his face.

'How did you get here to say goodbye?' I called out to him.

The Cuckoo Wizard shouted, 'Tickety-Boo! Enchanted magic of course!' and he winked at me.

The Snuggle-Buttons came over to join me and advised me,

'Keep your promises safe Jamie and always wear your bottle! We will miss you.'

As Mrs Snuggle-Button hugged me her nose wriggled around everywhere in this celebration.

I was just about to dwell on my feelings of sadness when Wisdom and Destiny jumped a few feet in front of me. They both were so huge that they almost squashed the Snuggle-Buttons whose noses were wriggling all over like crazy. Both Wisdom and Destiny rubbed my face with their wet noses. I understood what they were meaning. They were meaning 'Goodbye and we hope to see you again one day.'

Destiny hugged me with her huge floppy ears that were quite strong. We were special friends. After Destiny un-wrapped me from her ears I stepped back from all of my friends towards the Time-Keeper.

Shimmer from the group of Smithereens stepped forwards to say farewell,

'Our most precious guest,' she declared. 'It has been an honour to have you in our land and we only hope now that you will have a safe journey home. We will not forget you Jamie.'

Next the Watchers with their goggles on and colourful outfits stepped forwards to shake my hand. One by one they repeated

'Tood-a-loo!' 'Tood-a-loo!'

Just as they finished Orange came zooming from the air flapping her wings right in front of me. I jumped out of my skin, she was so fast. It was a terrific shock!

'Orange!' I roared 'You really do dive quickly!'

Orange replied,

'Jamie, I am most expert at my dives and landing if we spend more time together soon I will teach you how it is done! It takes no time whatsoever.'

I just hugged her tightly. My nose was tickled by the feathers everywhere,

'Thank you for being a true loyal friend Orange,' I declared.

The Time-Keeper stepped towards me and whispered into my ear

'It is now time for you to return home Jamie. You must return home now that the Challenge of Chime has been completed while you can. Nobody will enter our Enchanted Land of Bong again until there is another 'Twist of the Key.'

I nodded as we walked together side by side listening to what the Time-Keeper shared with me,

'For now the Time-Taker is banished back to his own planet or rather until our key is twisted again. Until then Jamie we all share in this victory.'

She looked deep into my brown eyes and I knew she was going to say something important,

'Jamie, it is important that what has happened here in the Enchanted Land of Bong must be kept between us as friends. You have the victory and it would be great for your friends at home know how you have won the Challenge of Chime.'

I nodded listening to each word.

She continued, 'I ask you not to share your adventure with others Jamie. A private victory in life is as magnificent and more powerful than a public one.'

I smiled at the Time-Keeper,

'I promise that I will keep the Enchanted Land of Bong safe and never tell anyone about my adventure.'

The Time-Keeper touched my face,

'You are a very special child Jamie with talents and gifts like nobody else. Always remember you are unique.'

I stood next to the massive key in the lock and the Time-Keeper stepped back as she announced,

'When we all shout to 'Twist the Key' Jamie.'

'You MUST twist the key.'

I held onto the key in the wooden window frame. Thankfully it was no longer red hot to touch. I was sorry to be leaving all of my new friends but I did want to get back home to the flamingo pink cottage and to my family. Suddenly, everyone shouted,

'TWIST THE KEY!' 'TWIST THE KEY!'

Using both hands and the whole of my body against the golden key I managed to push it around in the lock. It took all of my energy.

'CLICK!' The key turned.

'Whoosh, Whoop, Whoosh, Whoop. Tick-Tock Tick-Tock.'

'Whoosh, Whoop, Whoosh, Whoop, Tick-Tock, Tick-Tock.'

Once again there was beautiful music getting louder and all I could see was spirals and spirals of multi-coloured rainbows. Again they wrapped around the whole of my body. My feelings were like my body was being stretched out all over (a bit like hanging upside down from a tree by your feet) but throughout all of this I could hear,

'Whoosh. Whoop. Whoosh. Whoop. Whoosh. Whoop. Whoosh. Tick-Tock, Tick-Tock, Tick-Tock.'

'Whoosh. Whoop. Whoosh. Whoop. Whoosh. Whoop. Whoosh.

Tick-Tock, Tick-Tock, Tick-Tock.'

The Cog's beautiful music was playing louder and louder and it brought a huge smile on my face. I closed my eyes. It was so bright with rainbows flying past the front of my eyes I could not keep them open a moment longer. I could feel myself falling over backwards and at the same time I felt stretched like an elasticated rubber band. I must tell you it was the strangest feeling.

'BUMP!' I had landed onto soft flooring.

Ever so slowly I opened my eyes sensing that the brightness had turned into darkness. I could still hear the music playing softly in the background. There were no more rainbow spirals. There was just me on my own stretched out on Aunt Jane's beautiful Persian carpet. I was back at the flamingo pink cottage.

Chapter 22 - Home Sweet Home

'Jamie? Jamie? What on earth are you doing down here at this time of the night? Why are you sleeping on the floor Jamie?'

Aunt Jane stood on the staircase looking down at me. Before I spoke I looked at the Grandfather's Clock and could see that only a few hours had passed. How strange I thought. I was in that old clock for ages?

'I'm okay Aunt Jane. I just couldn't sleep and it is because I was worried about my parents,' I sighed.

I looked at the Grandfather's Clock; the key was back inside the lock. It still looked too large as it stuck out of the clock. Aunt Jane dashed down the stairs and knelt down beside me.

'Jamie, you must not worry. You know all will be well and you have me here whenever you need me. I am sure things will be fine including a speedy recovery,' she reassured.

We both stood up and went into the kitchen for a cup of Aunt Jane's hot chocolate delight (yes reader it does have little marshmallows on the top with a dusting of chocolate powder). According to Aunt Jane it is known to be the best sleeping remedy in the world,

'You cannot take one sip of my chocolate delight and stay awake!' she informed me.

At the table Aunt Jane mentioned,

'Tomorrow I would like us to all go together to a lovely little shop. It is in the village and it is ever so cute. I would like to get you and Emily a trinket to take home with you.'

Aunt Jane was beaming,

'This shop is fabulous as it has frogs that are bean-bags, sweet books and lots of cartoon character dolls.'

Now she had my interest and I smiled behind my massive cup of chocolate delight. Aunt Jane continued,

'I mean you know how much I love Cat-woman and frogs don't you!' She made me laugh. As an Auntie she was really like a child in a grown- up's body full of fun to relish.

'Aunt Jane that sounds really great to me. I am pretty sure Emily will love it too.'

As Aunt Jane took my cup away to wash up I noticed her little bottle sparkling on her necklace. Quickly I touched my neck beneath my pyjamas to check that my own gift from the Snuggle-Buttons was still there. Sure enough it was. I held the bottle and was looking at it when Aunt Jane turned to find me holding it in my hand. She walked over slowly with eyes wide open and sat down in the chair beside me. Aunt Jane was speechless. I was just looking at my bottle and the colours inside.

One day I will read my special promises from my bottle, I thought.

In a quiet voice she whispered, 'Some things must not be shared with others Jamie they are to be kept to oneself. If they are shared with others often they lose their special magic.'

I looked at Aunt Jane and she now was holding my bottle in the palm of her hand. She added with a smile,

'It is time for bed Jamie. We have a great day planned for tomorrow.'

I walked out of the kitchen and just before I climbed up the stairs I went to see the Grandfather's Clock once more. There in the wood was the engraved words GNOBLE. I ran my fingers over the letters and could feel the warmth in my fingertips as I did so,

'Enchanted Land of Bong,' I whispered.

Just as I started to climb the stairs I was sure I heard a Watcher's voice call to me,

'TOOD-A-LOO Jamie!'

From the staircase I could see both the Moon-Dial and Sun-Dial spinning perfectly around each other in the top of the Grandfather's Clock.

'Goodnight everyone,' I whispered.

Upstairs I climbed into bed feeling warm and blissful inside. Snuggled in bed, I looked at all of the glorious stars on the ceiling. What an adventure I thought. I closed my eyes and I just knew that everything happened for a reason.

In the morning I was woken up by voices and the smell of cookies baking. The aroma drifted into my bedroom and was so delicious it was not at all difficult to climb out of bed. After one stretch I ran downstairs and headed straight for the kitchen.

'Good morning Emily!' I smiled as she sat at the table slurping out of Aunt Jane's dotty cup.

Emily looked quite shocked at this point. In fact her eyes did look as though I had grown tentacles. She could not believe that I was being so nice and pleasant towards her. I then dived towards her and gave her a massive hug.

She said stunned,

'Morning Jamie. Aunt Jane is making cranberry and orange cookies.'

As I sat down at the table I felt something in my pyjama pocket scratch me. I put my hand into my pocket and there was the little sack of Gems that Gem-Star had given me. Aunt Jane and Emily were discussing the shapes of the cookies as I opened up the little sack. The beautiful gemstones sparkled. As I held them in my hands my whole body felt warm. I could not believe that I had not returned them to Gem-Star. Perhaps one day I will take them back to the Land of Bong, I thought.

Aunt Jane asked,

'Jamie would you like a cookie?' Quickly I put the gem stones back into my pocket.

'Two cookies please Aunt Jane,' I cheered.

After breakfast we whizzed out in the countryside in Aunt Jane's beetle. The roof was down as the weather was wonderful. The sun gleamed through the trees and there was a lovely breeze to keep us cool. We parked in the main square of Leyburn and jumped out of the car to follow Aunt Jane to this incredible shop she had found. Aunt Jane was wearing a beautiful dress and it had dots all over it with her perfect high heeled shoes. I've never seen Aunt Jane fall over in her heeled shoes yet, unlike my own mother.

As we entered the shop there was a little bell that sounded giving notice to the shop-keeper that we had entered. It did not take Emily long to run off leaving Aunt Jane and I to ponder. Disney princess dolls were on a shelf and Emily started her search immediately to find the best one she could as her present.

Sure enough the first toys I spotted were cute frogs that were beanbags. They had two types of material on them. Aunt Jane leaped with joy when she saw I'd found them.

'Don't you just love them Jamie,' she giggled.

In one swoop she picked up the frogs and declared that they were both going to a new home that very day. I laughed as Aunt Jane was more excited than Emily.

Soon enough I walked through to a sectioned part of the gift shop to find the most awesome toys. There under my nose were my favourite characters from different comic books. I read my comics every day. One by one I went through the toy characters and it was a real challenge for me to choose between Spiderman and Superman. Aunt Jane found me. She now was choosing between different masks for a superhero party she had been invited to.

'What do you think Jamie?' she asked holding a handful of masks. The decision was easy when she found a Cat-Woman mask.

'Here we are!' she announced putting the mask over her eyes, 'This is purr-fect!'

Shortly after which Aunt Jane took it to the counter.

As I held onto the two toys choosing which one was best. I looked up and there in front of me was a range of different Cuckoo Clocks! The birds were tweeting now and I called out,

'Aunt Jane. You must come and see these clocks. Come and see these clocks. They have real-living Cuckoos inside them! Could we get one of these please?'

Aunt Jane came into the room smiling,

'Now why would you want a Cuckoo Clock Jamie?' she asked.

From her smiling face I think she already knew why I wanted a Cuckoo Clock. My decision was made to purchase a Cuckoo-Clock and at the shop counter I asked the shop-keeper who was tidying the display unit, 'Excuse me. How did your delivery of Cuckoo Clocks arrive to this shop?'

The Shop-Keeper stopped tidying the display unit and he turned around. As I looked at his face he appeared so familiar. He winked at me and shocked I glanced down to see a red bow tie next to his name badge. It read 'Mr W. Izzard.'

He said perfectly calm, 'by extra special delivery of course!'

*THE END *

The Magical Land of Bong

'LOOK OVER THERE!' said Mrs Pendulum as she swung down to pass Mr Pendulum.

'What is it now?' Mr Pendulum asked.

'It is a G-I-R-L! Mr Bob. LOOK!' Mrs Pendulum was very excited and started to swing faster.

Mr Bob Pendulum swooped down again and lifted up his drooping moustache so he could take a clearer look at what his wife was talking about. Sure enough as Mr Pendulum took a careful inspection he saw a young girl with a surprised look on her face standing beneath them. She had a dotty dressing gown on, slippers to match with long curly brown hair. Her mouth was wide open as she appeared totally stunned.

'How do you do and what is your name?' Mrs Pendulum asked.

'My name is Jane, How do you do? I have no idea where I am?' the young girl answered.

'We are Splendid! Thank you,' said Mr Pendulum.

'Welcome to the Enchanted Land of Bong!' said Mrs Pendulum as she swooped past Jane. 'You have been chosen as our *GUEST*!

Jane was looking forward to a traditional Christmas and staying with her Grandparents in London with her sister Julia. On Christmas Eve Jane is drawing the old Grandfather's Clock in the library. Until she 'Twists a Key' in the lock of the wooden clock that takes her on a magical adventure. Jane makes friends with Scamper the Fur-Fog and the Snuggle-Buttons who in turn must rescue Jane from the Time-Taker who is determined for Jane to never return home.

About the Author

At the age of ten Charlotte Jones visited her school friend's house and was fascinated by a magnificent old Grandfather's Clock. In that moment of curiosity the story of The Enchanted Grandfather's Clock was created clearly with all the characters and plots.

Charlotte is from Darlington in the North-East of England and is a Qualified Nurse, Teacher, Coach and Author. During her college years she spent much time in North Yorkshire visiting places in this book in the midst of strawberry picking and of course the 'Tea-pot Trail.'

She attended a writer's circle at seventeen and was encouraged to write this story.

Interestingly, Charlotte adores pet rabbits the character Cat-Woman and cute V.W. Beetle cars. She loves hosting Pudding Parties, Murder Mystery Parties and spending fun times with family and friends.

Acknowledgements

Each and every one of us is comparable to the tiny seed that gets planted into the ground. Each seed has huge opportunity to grow if we are watered and cared for. We must not forget those delightful rays of sunshine that beam over that dedicated earth or the drops of water that replenish it. Combined ~ it all creates the perfect place to grow.

It is not extraordinary for me to say that in life we are as good as those who coach and teach us. Those who take on that role to guide us are in a position of privilege. They serve others and there is something so special about people who love to help others achieve their goals.

Magnificent coaches move us in becoming our best and to overcome fears. One of my coaches helped me to jump off a 60 foot pole. I had a fear of heights until the moment I jumped!

I am so blessed that all of my teachers and coaches inspired me in my life to believe that the impossible can be possible.

For many years this story was just a bedtime story read to my child who truly brought my characters to life. It was a story written and unpublished on a computer for far too long!

This book published is from my heart.

'*Thank you,*' to those for being with me on my journey to be where I am right now in this moment,

My Dad Reggie ~ the greatest encourager

Avril English ~ inspiring me to publish my book

Parisa Jones ~ for loving my characters and creating them in reality

Victoria Bond ~ for listening

Stephanie Hale ~ my publisher for her wisdom and her belief in my stories

Robert F. Moore ~ a motivational speaker who moves me!

Michael Carroll ~ for his teaching of excellence in the centre of the universe

'Bula!' to my Robbins Life Mastery family 2013 and our coaches

In particular, Loren Slocum and Michael Savage, these precious people helped me to find true purpose and my own understanding in *'why'* this book and sharing my stories was a *'must'* for me.

My Readers ~ I hope you enjoy the story.

Charlotte Jones x